W9-CBQ-051

DANCE DIVAS

Step It Up

DANCE DIVAS

Showtime!

Two to Tango

Let's Rock!

Step It Up

On Pointe
(coming soon)

DANCE DIVAS

Step It Up

Sheryl Berk

BLOOMSBURY
NEW YORK LONDON NEW DELHI SYDNEY

First published in the United States of America in September 2014
by Bloomsbury Children's Books
www.bloomsbury.com

Library of Congress Cataloging-in-Publication Data
Berk, Sheryl.
Step it up / by Sheryl Berk.
pages cm — (Dance Divas ; 4)
Summary: Trouble is brewing between the Divas just before their big upcoming Dance Fusion competition. Miss Toni is mad, mad, mad—but she has an idea to fix the problem: a camping retreat, where these girls will have to learn the true meaning of teamwork or be left out in the dark.
ISBN 978-1-61963-583-8 (paperback) • ISBN 978-1-61963-582-1 (hardcover)
ISBN 978-1-61963-584-5 (e-book)
[1. Dance teams—Fiction. 2. Dance—Fiction. 3. Interpersonal relations—Fiction.] I. Title.
PZ7.B45236St 2014 [Fic]—dc23 2014009650

Book design by Donna Mark
Typeset by Westchester Book Composition
Printed and bound in the U.S.A. by Thomson-Shore Inc., Dexter, Michigan
2 4 6 8 10 9 7 5 3 1 (paperback)
2 4 6 8 10 9 7 5 3 1 (hardcover)

To my bestie Holly Gates Russell

You are my rock

Love, Sherelle

Table of Contents

1	Sibling Rivalry	1
2	The Queen of the Team	9
3	The Name Game	15
4	Monkey See, Monkey Do	21
5	Seeing Double	32
6	Let the Games Begin!	42
7	Roll with It	50
8	It's a Jungle out There	60
9	Toni's Test	69
10	Ready to Rough It	80
11	Camp Diva	84
12	Not-So-Happy Trails	94
13	Carried Away	103
14	A Bewitching Tale	113
15	Whooooo Goes There?	123
16	Bouncing Back	130
	Glossary of Dance Terms	137

DANCE DIVAS

Step It Up

CHAPTER 1

Sibling Rivalry

Scarlett Borden rummaged through her dresser drawer searching for a pair of pink ballet tights for class. She was sure she'd seen them in there just yesterday. There were leg warmers, shorts, harem pants . . .

"Mom," she called. "Did you take my pink mesh tights?"

Her mother poked her head into Scarlett's room. She had a handful of student papers she was grading, and her reading glasses were perched on the tip of her nose.

"Honey, why would I take your tights?" she

said and sighed. “Do I look like one of the Dance Divas to you?”

Scarlett had to chuckle. The image of her mom on a girls competitive dance team was pretty silly. She could just imagine her trying to do a *grand jeté* with bent knees across their kitchen!

“Um, guess not,” Scarlett answered. “No offense . . .”

“None taken,” her mother replied. “My feet hurt enough from standing in front of a classroom all day. I can’t imagine being *en pointe*!”

Scarlett continued searching in her dance bag. “I just can’t understand where they could have gone. I swear I had them when Gracie came in my room and asked me to help get her Monopoly game from the closet.”

Just then, a thought popped into Scarlett’s head: Where had Gracie been while she was climbing on a step stool to reach the top shelf of the hall closet?

“Excuse me, Mom,” Scarlett said. “I think I know who took my tights.”

She stormed into Gracie's bedroom. Her little sister was sitting on the floor, surrounded by a pile of Barbie dolls. "*Shhh!*" Gracie held up a finger to her lips. "This is the final round of the Miss Beautiful Doll Pageant. It's the interview."

She waved a Barbie in the air and pretended to speak for her in a Southern twang. "Y'all should vote for me! If I'm crowned Miss Beautiful Doll, I will save all the trees and the oceans. Oh, and the pigs!" She held up her favorite plush pink pig, Petunia, the one she tucked into bed every night.

Scarlett shook her head. "I didn't know pigs were endangered."

"Hello? Do you know how many people eat pork chops and bacon?" Gracie replied. "I vow to save all the piggies of the world!"

Scarlett had just about enough of Gracie's silly games. "I want my tights back," she insisted and held out her palm. "Now."

"I don't have your tights, Scoot," Gracie said. "What would I want with your dumb old tights anyway?"

Out of the corner of her eye, Scarlett caught a glimpse of one of Gracie's dolls. She was wearing a makeshift pink strapless gown, dotted with red nail-polish polka dots. It looked vaguely familiar.

"Is that . . . ?" she began, and reached for the doll.

"No!" Gracie scooped it up before she could get to it. She hid it behind her back.

"Gracie, let me see that doll's dress," Scarlett said, gritting her teeth.

"Nuh-uh!" Gracie insisted. "I worked really hard on that pageant gown. You can't have it."

Scarlett knew it was no use trying to wrestle it out of her hands. Gracie was quick—and slippery. She needed to be smart.

"Okay, whatever," she said. "I don't want your doll."

"You don't?" Gracie asked.

"Nope. I want Petunia!" She grabbed Gracie's favorite stuffed animal and held it high in the air. "Hand over the Barbie or Petunia takes a swim in the toilet bowl."

"You wouldn't!" Gracie howled. "I'll tell!"

"Tell all you want. She'll be soaking wet and flushed by then."

"Mommy!" Gracie yelled.

Scarlett walked toward the doorway. "I hope Petunia knows how to piggy paddle . . ."

"Okay! Okay!" Gracie finally gave in. "You can have the doll. Just give me back my pig."

They swapped, and Scarlett took a close look at the doll's dress. It was pink mesh—just like her tights. "Gracie, how could you?" Scarlett gasped. "You cut up my tights?"

Gracie nibbled her nails. "I needed something pretty for the evening-gown round," she said. "You can have 'em back." She handed Scarlett the tights she had hidden under her bed. One foot was missing.

"What am I supposed to do with those now? I can't wear that to class with Miss Toni!"

Scarlett's dance teacher freaked if she had a single snag in her tights. She couldn't imagine what she'd think of a pair missing an entire foot.

"You are *so* buying me a new pair!" Scarlett shouted.

"I don't have any money!"

"What about your piggy bank?" Scarlett asked. "Gram always fills it with spare change when she comes to visit."

Gracie stamped her feet. "That's *my* money. I'm saving up for a Barbie Beach Cruiser."

This time it was Scarlett's turn to tattle. "Mom!" she called downstairs. "Gracie ruined my ballet tights!"

"Work it out, girls," their mother shouted from her home office. She was up to her ears in papers that needed to be graded.

"You're too old to be playing with Barbies!" Scarlett shouted at her sister. "Dolls are for babies."

"I'm not a baby!" Gracie yelled.

"You're a baby . . . and a tights thief," Scarlett fired back.

"Oh yeah? Well, you don't even know what I did with your red leotard!"

Scarlett gasped. "My red leotard? The one I wore for the 'Gotta Have Heart' number at Rising Stars?" She remembered it well: it was a beautiful crimson velvet with gold studs around the neckline. She'd taken first place in the Junior Solo category when she wore it. "You'd better not have put my leotard on some stupid Barbie!"

Gracie smiled. "I didn't put it on a Barbie." She pointed to the corner of her room where she had staged a procession of dolls walking on a red carpet.

"You cut up my leotard to make a red carpet?" Scarlett fumed. "Gracie, this is the last straw!" She began chasing her little sister around the room. Gracie screamed.

"Okay, that's enough!" Their mother appeared in the doorway to referee. "You girls have got to learn to stop fighting!"

She turned to Gracie. "You will pay your sister back for her tights and leotard out of your allowance," she said sternly. "As long as it takes you to do so."

"And you," she said, facing Scarlett, "will stop picking on Gracie."

Both girls pouted.

"Now if you don't mind, I have papers to grade." She looked at her watch. "And Scarlett, you have fifteen minutes to get to ballet class."

"Without tights?" Scarlett sighed. "Miss Toni is going to kill me!"

CHAPTER 2

The Queen of the Team

Scarlett made it to ballet class just seconds before her teacher shut the door of studio 3.

"Sorry, Miss Toni," she said, panting. She silently prayed Miss Toni wouldn't notice that her tights were "mocha" and not "theater pink."

Toni furrowed her brow. If there was one thing she couldn't tolerate, it was tardiness. "Start stretching," she told Scarlett. "Everyone else is warmed up already."

Scarlett took her place at the *barre* next to Anya, Rochelle, Bria, and Liberty. Rochelle shot her a concerned look.

"Don't ask," Scarlett whispered. "Hurricane Gracie turned my tights and leotard into a *Project Runway* episode."

Rochelle laughed. "I know it's not funny . . . but it's kinda funny."

"We're just lucky she's not old enough to be in pointe class with us," Anya said.

Tell me about it, Scarlett thought. It was hard enough having a pesky little sister at home. But Gracie was also an official member of the Dance Divas Elite Competition Team, and that meant that every day, at every rehearsal for a competition, she was there to drive her crazy. Her only Gracie-free zone was the more advanced pointe class.

"Straighten that supporting knee!" Toni barked as Scarlett ran through the warm-up. "Tuck your butt in and stand up straight in that roll-up!" Scarlett glanced in the mirror: her arch *did* look less than spectacular. And she struggled to keep up with the combination. "Scarlett, are you on another planet today?" Toni said. "Those feet should be in fifth position!"

By the end of the class, Scarlett had fallen into sync with the others, but Toni was still eyeing her. "You're all dismissed—except for Scarlett," she said.

"Uh-oh," Bria whispered. "That's never a good thing."

"Maybe she wants to talk to you about a solo at Dance Fusion?" Anya suggested. Scarlett had almost forgotten about their competition two weeks from Saturday. Toni had yet to tell any of them the details of what they'd be dancing—only that their rival team, City Feet, would be competing as well.

"Maybe she wants to kick your butt off the team?" Liberty smirked.

Scarlett gulped. Miss Toni had been pretty hard on her the entire class. Was she mad enough to ban her from the next competition? Or worse, from being a Diva? She was always threatening to replace anyone who didn't "toe the line."

"Miss Toni loves you," Rochelle assured her. "You're our best dancer!"

Liberty picked up her dance bag and tossed it

over her shoulder. "You mean she *used* to be our best dancer. Now that title belongs to me."

Rochelle bristled. "Says who? I don't see anyone handing you a crown, Liberty. Unless your rich mommy, the big-time Hollywood choreographer, bought you one?"

Rochelle knew how much Liberty hated when people accused her of being successful because of her mom's connections. The truth was, Liberty worked just as hard as any of the Divas. She had an attitude, but she could dance. Still, it was fun to push her buttons.

Scarlett put her hand on Rochelle's shoulder. "Rock, that's enough," she said softly. She knew that Liberty loved to brag, but underneath it was a lot of hurt and insecurity—especially when it came to her mother.

Liberty stormed out of the studio. "You guys better go, too," Scarlett said. "I'll let you know how it goes." She walked over to Miss Toni, who was busy jotting notes on her clipboard.

"You want to talk to me?" she said nervously.

"Yes, I do." Toni didn't bother to glance up from her work. "I assume your appearance and your performance today were a one-time scenario?"

"Yes! Absolutely! I'm so sorry! Gracie was just driving me nuts right before I got here. She gave her Barbie my tights and, oh my gosh, my leotard is now a red carpet . . ."

Toni put down her pen. "Are you and Gracie not getting along?"

"Well, she's kind of a pain," Scarlett tried to explain. "I mean, she just has no respect for me or my things."

Toni nodded. "You know how I feel about fighting on my team," she said firmly. "Anyone who can't get along with her teammates cannot be a Diva."

Scarlett held her breath. *Here it comes*, she thought. Liberty was right; she was kicking her off the team.

"That said," Toni continued, "I think I have a solution." She got up from her stool and went to the corner of the studio where she'd placed a small cardboard box. She carried it over and placed it at Scarlett's feet.

"I think you and your little sister need something to remind you what it is to be loving and caring. Something you can do together."

Scarlett had no idea what she was talking about, but she did notice that the box had several large, round holes punched out of its side.

"Go on," Toni said. "Open it."

Scarlett knelt down and lifted the lid. Inside was a ball of orange fur. "A kitten!" she exclaimed, scooping it into her arms. It was so small, she could practically fit it in the palm of her hand.

"My neighbor had a litter. I asked your mother, and she said you can have one—as long as you and Gracie promise to take good care of him."

"Oh, I will! We will!" Scarlett said, stroking the tiny kitten. "He's so sweet! Thank you, Miss Toni!"

"You're welcome." Toni almost smiled. "Just don't ever come to my class again in mocha tights."

CHAPTER 3

The Name Game

Scarlett couldn't wait to get home and show the kitten to Gracie.

"Isn't he precious?" she said, scratching him behind the ears.

"You girls have to think of a name for him," her mother pointed out. "And you have to set up his bed and litter box."

Scarlett nodded. "I think we should call him Baryshnikov—after the famous ballet dancer."

Gracie made a gagging sound. "That's a terrible name for a cute little kitty." She snatched the cat from Scarlett's hands. "We don't like that name do we?" she asked the cat, cradling him in her arms. "I think we should name you Mr. Mustard."

"Mustard?" Scarlett exclaimed. "You might as well name him Hot Dog! Or Ketchup!"

"Oooh, I like Kitty Ketchup for a name," Gracie said. "But I think Mr. Mustard is perfect. He's the color of mustard, don't ya think?"

Scarlett looked to her mother for help. "You're not going to let her name our cat after a condiment, are you?" she pleaded. "It's the stupidest name I've ever heard!"

"I am not stupid!" Gracie piped up. "Your Bar-fish-no-cough name is just as dumb. Cats can't dance ballet!"

Their mother sighed and took the kitten from Gracie. "Look, if the two of you can't get along and give this cat a loving home, I am giving the cat back to Miss Toni. End of argument."

Scarlett looked at the tiny kitten. He looked so helpless. How could she let him go? "Fine." She sighed. "We can call him Mr. Mustard—for now. Until we think of something better."

"Yay!" Gracie squealed.

Her mother placed the cat back in Scarlett's lap. "I think you've made a wise decision."

Scarlett glared at her little sister. Why did Gracie always have to win? Just because she was younger didn't give her the right to always get her way.

"Hello, Mr. Mustard," Gracie cooed. "Who's a pretty kitty?"

The next afternoon at the Dance Divas Studio, Gracie couldn't wait to share the news of their new pet with her teammates. "And we named him Mr. Mustard!" she told Rochelle and Bria in the dressing room.

Rochelle shot Scarlett a look. "*We* named him that?"

"Please," Scarlett grumped, "don't get me started. I wanted to call him Baryshnikov or Joffrey or Balanchine. But my mom said we had to agree or we couldn't keep him."

Gracie skipped off to find Miss Toni and give her a report.

"It could be worse," Bria said, trying to cheer her up. "She could have named him Grey Poupon."

"It's not funny." Scarlett sighed. She had just about had it with Gracie acting spoiled and getting away with it. Even Miss Toni gave her special treatment.

When Gracie wobbled on a *pirouette* a few days ago and fell on the floor, Scarlett thought for sure Toni would launch into a lecture about the importance of spotting and balance. Instead, she helped Gracie to her feet and suggested she picture her favorite gymnast, Gabby Douglas, standing in the front of the room. "Look right into Gabby's eyes," she told her. "Concentrate on that one spot." It took Gracie about a dozen tries to get it right, and when she did, Miss Toni high-fived her.

"None of us get any sympathy if we fall on our butts," Scarlett said. "Much less a high five. I don't get it. Why is Gracie always the favorite?"

Rochelle shrugged. "'Cause she's younger. The first time my baby brother, Dylan, pooped in his diaper, my mom and dad jumped for joy and told him he was a genius. All he did was poop!"

"Little kids always get more attention—that's just how it is," Bria added.

"You're a little sister. I don't see you behaving like that and driving your sister up the wall," Scarlett pointed out.

"That's because my sister *is* a genius—and I don't mean at pooping." Bria laughed. "I always feel like I have to compete with her. Maybe that's how Gracie feels around you."

Scarlett thought it over. That might have been the case a few months ago, when she was winning trophies for dance. But now they were both Divas, dancing on the same team, and Gracie was getting better by the day. It had been Scarlett's idea to ask Miss Toni to let Gracie join the team—her tumbling was pretty awesome after all. Had she created a monster?

"What do you always tell me when Liberty is making me nuts?" Rochelle asked her.

Scarlett recalled the last time she had to seriously referee her teammates. Liberty decided that Rochelle's jazz shoes "needed freshening." So she put them outside on the windowsill during a torrential downpour. When Rochelle found them, they were a soggy mess and the soles were falling off.

"I think I told her she should mind her own shoe business?" Scarlett said. "And I believe I stopped you from sticking her head under the faucet as payback?"

Rochelle nodded. "I still say her face needed freshening . . . but I saw your point. Two wrongs don't make a right."

Scarlett nodded. "So you're saying I should forget the whole Mr. Mustard thing and move on?"

Bria pointed to the clock. "We all need to move—five minutes till rehearsal!"

CHAPTER 4

Monkey See, Monkey Do

The girls rushed into the studio the next day and began stretching. Gracie squeezed in beside Scarlett at the *barre*. "I told Miss Toni and she loves the name Mr. Mustard," she whispered. "She said it was really cute and clever."

Scarlett gritted her teeth and tried to focus on her *cambre back*. Maybe if she ignored Gracie, she'd go away and stop bugging her.

"Okay, time to talk Dance Fusion," Toni said, taking her place on a tall stool at the front of the room. "This is a big competition in Connecticut, and I want to pull out all the stops."

"What else is new?" Rochelle muttered under her breath.

"Rochelle and Liberty," Toni said, "I am putting you two together in a duet."

Liberty's face went pale. "A duet? With *her*? *Again?*"

"Is there a problem? Because I'm happy to give Rochelle a solo if you're not up for it," Toni said, warning her.

"Fine," Liberty grumped. "I'll do it." She turned to Rochelle. "I'm not about to let you have a solo."

"It's called 'Going Bananas,' " Toni continued. "It's an acro routine and you're going to wear this." She tossed Rochelle a bright yellow leotard.

"OMG, that is hideous!" Liberty said. "I'll look like a giant highlighter pen!"

"Oh no. That's not your costume," their coach replied. "This is yours." She handed Liberty a brown, fuzzy unitard with a long tail attached.

Liberty's face turned bright red. Scarlett

actually thought she saw steam coming out of her ears. "No way! I am not making a fool out of myself in that!"

"What's the matter?" Rochelle taunted her. "Afraid of a little monkey business on the dance floor?"

"This is going to get ugly." Anya sighed. "I can see it coming."

"I refuse to wear this—and to dance with that," Liberty fumed. "I'm gonna tell my mother. She will never stand for it."

Toni stayed cool as a cucumber. "Then take a seat, Liberty," she said calmly. "In the corner, on the mat. No one is forcing you to dance on the Divas team."

She turned back to the class. "Bria and Anya, you're also doing a duet. It's a lyrical routine called 'Count the Stars,' and I'm going to need your moms to help with the costuming."

"My mom's totally into it," Bria volunteered. "She's a whiz at BeDazzling."

Anya wrinkled her nose. "BeDazzling? I was

thinking more simple and classic like the night sky . . ."

Toni held up her hand. "Girls, the costumes are the least of my concerns at the moment. We need to block out the group routine today."

She went to the closet and pulled out a large inflated beach ball. She tossed it to Scarlett. "I call this number 'By the Beautiful Sea.' You're all going to be 1920s bathing beauties frolicking on the seashore."

Gracie's hand went up. "Miss Toni, can I be the one in the bathtub?" she asked, hopefully.

Scarlett sighed. "Gracie, there is no bathtub. It's set on the beach."

"In hideously ugly costumes with bloomers," Liberty piped up from the corner. "As if the monkey suit wasn't bad enough."

Miss Toni ignored the chatter. "I've found real vintage bathing suits for all of you—and parasols and bathing caps."

She held up a black-and-white photo of a woman in a navy-and-white striped skirted bathing suit with baggy white bloomers peeking out from underneath.

Gracie stared at the image. "I don't get it. How's she gonna swim in that? Can't we just wear bikinis?"

Liberty's hand shot up. "I second bikinis!"

Scarlett actually thought she heard Toni growl. "I have had enough of all of you today," she said firmly. "The only voice I want to hear now is my own. Is that clear?"

Six heads nodded in unison. Toni meant business.

"I want two lines of three. Scarlett, Gracie, Rochelle. You're up front. Anya, Bria, you're in the back. And Liberty, too . . . if you care to grace us with your presence?"

Liberty stood up and took her place in line.

"This number is nostalgic. It will be light and lively with lots of kicks and tricks. I want the judges to be wowed from the minute you set foot onstage."

She motioned for Scarlett to toss her the

beach ball. "This is going to be in constant motion during the routine, passing from hand to hand." She tossed it at Rochelle, who was caught off guard and nearly dropped it.

"Anyone who is not on the ball for this group number will have me to deal with."

* * *

Rochelle wasn't sure that Liberty would show up for their duet rehearsal the next day. She could have kissed Miss Toni for making Liberty the monkey instead of her. How funny would she look jumping around onstage and shaking her tail?

When Liberty walked into the studio, Rock had to try her hardest not to crack up. She knew Toni wouldn't tolerate it.

"Oh, so you've decided to join us?" Toni asked Liberty. "If you're going to do this duet, I don't want any complaining—not about your dance, not about your costume, and not about this . . ." She put a pair of monkey ears on top of Liberty's bun. Rochelle burst out laughing. This was payback for her soaked shoes and every snarky comment Liberty had ever made!

"This is ridiculous!" Liberty cried. "We're going to be the laughingstocks of Dance Fusion!"

"Not if I have anything to say about it," Toni assured her. "You're going to stop the show."

She demonstrated what she wanted them to do: Rochelle would roll across the stage and Liberty would leap and flip over her. The timing had to be perfectly synchronized. There was not a split second to hesitate or make a mistake. It was some of the most complicated choreography Toni had ever created for them.

"You gotta admit it's a pretty cool dance," Rochelle said to Liberty as they tossed their bags on a bench in the dressing room. Gracie was already there, getting ready to run through the group routine.

Liberty shrugged. "Whatevs. It's not any cooler than what my mom just choreographed for a hot, new pop star."

"Toni knows what she's doing." Rochelle

couldn't believe the words coming out of her mouth. Wasn't she the one who was always questioning her coach's out-of-the-box ideas? Amazingly, she was learning to trust her; they all were. Except maybe Liberty.

"I would have gone for sequins—chocolate-brown velvet with gold sequins," she said. "Not fuzz."

"Fuzz is fun," Gracie piped up. "My cat, Mr. Mustard, is fuzzy."

Liberty continued to fume. "Please do not compare me to your raggedy feline," she said. "If you're going to call me an animal, at least make it a mink . . . or a chinchilla."

Oh, great, Rochelle thought to herself, *that's just what we need: for Liberty to turn this dance number into a chinchilla chasing a banana!*

"Don't pick on my kitty," Gracie said, pointing her finger in Liberty's face. "You take that back."

Liberty smirked. "Take what back?"

"What you called Mr. Mustard. A Raggedy Ann sea lion."

Rochelle couldn't help but giggle. Gracie had quite a way with words.

"And don't laugh at me, Rock!" the little girl shouted at her. "It's not funny!"

She ran out of the dressing room, practically knocking Bria over on her way in.

"What was that about?" she asked.

Liberty shrugged. "Grace Face tantrum. Nothing new."

"Because you insulted her kitten," Rochelle reminded her. "You can't just tell everybody off because you feel like it. Right, Bria?"

Bria looked up, startled. She hated to take sides. "Um, I guess?"

"All I said was my costume could be a little more stylish," Liberty explained.

Bria bit her lip. "Maybe Liberty has a point? I'm kinda partial to sequins and BeDazzling myself."

Anya walked in and overheard them. "Tell me about it. My costume looks like the Milky Way exploded." She held up the leotard that Bria and her mom had adorned. Every inch was covered in silver and gold stars. "Bria, this is hideous."

"It's gorgeous!" Bria insisted. "We're supposed to sparkle and shine."

"Sparkle and shine, yes. Blind the audience, not so much."

"There's no such thing as too much sparkle," Liberty interrupted. "You just have to be dazzling enough to carry it off. A plain Jane can't handle it."

Anya's eyes narrowed. "Did you just call me a plain Jane?"

Liberty smirked. "Would you prefer Ordinary Anya?"

"I'd prefer you to zip your lip," Anya warned her.

"I'd prefer you all to zip your lips," said a voice at the doorway. It was Toni, and she looked furious. "I could hear you yelling all the way down the hall in studio one with the door shut."

Gracie peeked out behind her. "I told you,

Miss Toni," she tattled. "She started it!" She pointed straight at Liberty.

"And I'm finishing it," Toni fumed. "I don't know what's gotten into all of you, but if I hear any more bickering, I'll start replacing the Divas. Is that clear?"

Scarlett walked into the dressing room just as Miss Toni was storming out.

"Whoa! What did I miss?" she asked Rochelle.

"A major Toni meltdown," Rock replied. "And a warning: get along or get off the team."

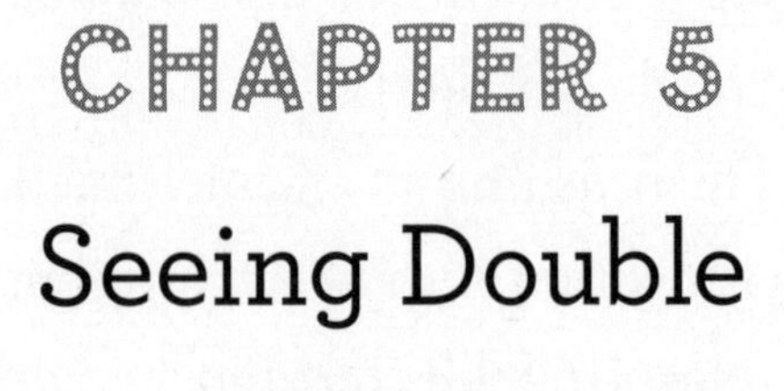

CHAPTER 5
Seeing Double

Dance Fusion was one of the biggest dance competitions in the tristate area and a showcase for the best and brightest studios. As the Divas filed onto the bus, Toni sat in the front seat, reviewing her notes for each number.

"She's going to switch something, I can feel it in my bones," Rochelle whispered to Scarlett. Her teacher had a bad habit of reworking dances en route to every competition and springing it on them just as they arrived.

"Maybe she's finally come to her senses and recast the duet," Liberty said, kicking her feet up on the back of Rock's seat. "Anyone can see you're more of a monkey than I am."

Scarlett didn't even have to remind her of Miss Toni's warning. "I know, I know," Rochelle said. "Ignore her."

Liberty smiled—she loved it when Rock couldn't argue back. "Try not to slip up onstage, Rock," she added. "That would drive Toni *bananas*."

Scarlett suspected it would be a long ride, especially with everyone stressed and angry at each other. Bria was barely talking to Anya. Anya was hardly talking to Liberty. And Liberty was furious at Rock. As for her and Gracie, they'd somehow managed to forgive and forget over the kitten's name. But there was still the matter of Gracie getting into her stuff.

"That's funny. I can't find my pink lip gloss," Scarlett said, searching through her makeup bag.

Rochelle elbowed her. "You mean that one?" Gracie was happily seated two rows behind them, slicking a wand across her lips.

"Gracie, give that back!" Scarlett called to her. "That's mine, not yours!"

Gracie quickly hid the tube behind her back. "I don't have anything," she fibbed.

"Then why are your lips so pink and shiny?" Scarlett asked. She was about to pounce on her little sister and retrieve her lip gloss when Rock stopped her.

"Remember what Toni said: get along or get off the team."

When they reached the venue, Miss Toni led them off the bus. "I want to remind everyone to be on their best behavior. City Feet is in the house, and that's never a good thing."

She'd barely finished her sentence when a second bus pulled up in front of theirs. Justine Chase, the coach of City Feet and Toni's frenemy, waved from the window.

"Oh boy. Here we go," Rochelle said.

The bus door opened and the girls bounded down the steps. There was Addison, Phoebe, Regan, and Mandy—aka "the Tiny Terror." Rock braced herself and waited for their competitors to taunt them with their obnoxious comments. Instead, the team filed past them without a single word. Not even Justine said anything.

"Okay, that was weird," Liberty remarked. "I was totally prepared to put that mean little munchkin, Mandy, in her place."

"That is how a team carries itself," Toni explained. "Strong and united. They don't have to mouth off because they know how good they are."

"Or Mandy ran out of one-liners from her insult book," Liberty said.

"Or has a mouth full of peanut butter and her lips are glued shut." Bria giggled.

"Whatever the reason, City Feet just showed you up with their poise and confidence," Toni said. "I suggest you all march in and follow their lead."

* * *

The convention center in Bristol, Connecticut, was teeming with dance groups from all over the country. Scarlett spotted a few they'd gone up against before: the Fab 5 from Philly, the Hippie Chicks from New Hampshire, and the Groovy Boyz from Long Island.

"This competition is fierce," she whispered to her teammates. "Did you see the Hippie Chicks? They came with a giant neon peace sign!"

"It's just a prop," Anya assured them. "I'm sure our dance is way cooler."

"Don't you mean way lamer?" Liberty said. "Bathing beauties. Puh-lease!"

When they found Miss Toni to run their dances by her one last time, she was busy blowing up their giant beach ball with a bicycle pump.

"I know how that beach ball feels," Liberty said and tugged on her bloomers.

"It's not *so* bad," Scarlett said, adjusting the white ruffled hat on her head. "I mean, it's comfortable." The bathing suit itself was a navy belted dress with a white sailor collar and matching navy-and-white striped bloomers.

"Speak for yourself," Anya complained. Her suit had lacy trim around the puffy sleeves. "This thing is itchy!"

Gracie's costume was the most colorful: a red-and-white polka dot one-piece with white bow trim and a matching red cap. "I don't get it. Why did people used to swim in their pajamas?" she asked.

Toni ignored them and applied her red lipstick in the dressing room mirror. She smoothed her black hair back into a bun and made sure every hair was in place.

"I just wish we knew what Stinky Feet was doing for the group dance," Rochelle said. "They were way too quiet. They definitely have something up their sleeves."

Bria flipped through the competition program. When she saw the name of their group dance, her eyes grew wide. "Guys, you better come look at this," she said.

Liberty grabbed the booklet out of her hands. "Lemme see that," she said. She read out loud: "City Feet will be performing 'Don't Be a Diva,' a contemporary jazz routine."

Rochelle's jaw dropped. "They've gotta be kidding! That is such a diss!"

Toni clapped her hands to silence them. "Enough. If they want to take a swipe at us, let them. Imitation is the sincerest form of flattery." Scarlett could sense a story coming on.

"Did I ever tell you about the time Justine wore my dress to the Ballet Gala?" she asked the girls.

"No," Rochelle muttered under her breath, "but I'm sure you're gonna."

"I had picked out this beautiful white gown with pearl beading at the waist," she continued. "The saleswoman assured me it was one-of-a-kind, and I was so excited to wear it. I left it at the store to be shortened."

Liberty's hand shot up. "Let me guess: Justine found an identical dress and wore it to the party to embarrass you? That is so tacky!"

"Worse," Toni said. "Like I said, it was one-of-a-kind. She went to the store and convinced the saleswoman she was there to pick up the dress for me. When I went back to the boutique, the woman who helped me said 'my friend' had come to get it since I was 'sick.' I couldn't find Justine anywhere . . . until she walked into the gala wearing my dress."

Scarlett gasped. "You must have been devastated!"

Toni shook her head. "No, I found another gown that was even prettier—a pale pink one with a beaded rhinestone bodice. I could have yelled at Justine for taking my dress, but I didn't. I realized how insecure she was, and I felt sorry for her."

"I would have dunked her head in the punch bowl," Rochelle said. "That was low, really low."

"Maybe so," Toni replied. "But there's always a positive way to look at something that's negative. Just remember that today when City Feet goes out there and does their number." She gathered her bag and clipboard and held the door of the dressing room open. "Everybody out. Game faces on. And, Anya, that bathing hat is on backward."

Anya turned the cap around till the big, floppy bow was hanging in her eyes. "How can you tell?"

They walked into the backstage waiting area and Toni gave them a last-minute warning before taking her seat in the audience. "Do not embarrass me."

Liberty waited until she was out of earshot. "She's kidding, right? How embarrassing are these costumes? We look like turn-of-the-century marshmallows. I'm sure City Feet will be all sparkled and sequined and glammed up."

Bria elbowed her. "Not exactly."

The girls looked behind them to see the City Feet team making their way toward the stage. Scarlett gasped. "Oh no!"

Addison, Phoebe, Regan, and Mandy were dressed in black shorts and black-and-hot pink satin bomber jackets that looked a lot like the Divas' team jackets. They were wearing black wigs styled in tight buns and bright red lipstick. Gracie said what they were all thinking out loud. "They all look just like Miss Toni!"

"No wonder they kept their mouths shut when they saw us," Rochelle whispered. "They were planning an ambush! We have to do something!"

But it was too late. The announcer had already taken his spot at the podium. "Ladies and gentlemen, we're ready to begin. Please welcome the first team in the Junior Group Dance category. City Feet from Long Island!"

CHAPTER 6

Let the Games Begin!

Addison stepped out on the stage carrying a stool. She placed it in the corner and took a seat, crossing her legs and pretending to take notes in an imaginary notebook. The rest of the girls filed in and took their place in a straight line in front of her. As the music started, they marched around the room like soldiers in perfect synchronization, with their arms and legs straight.

"Okay, this is creeping me out," Bria said, peeking out from the wings to watch them.

One by one, each of the girls shed her jacket to reveal a hot pink sequined crop top.

"I told you," Liberty said. "Sequins!"

Then they unpinned their buns and let their hair flow free. Mandy did a perfect roundoff back handspring while Phoebe and Regan did *fouettés* around her. Finally, Addison—who was clearly playing the part of Toni—clapped her hands together and the music came to an abrupt stop. She pointed to each of the girls, and they became "soldiers" once again. She gave the audience an intimidating stare before the lights onstage went black.

"I don't get it," Gracie said. "Was she trying to be a mean Toni?" The audience and the judges didn't quite know what to make of the whole thing. There was a long pause before they applauded.

"Where is Toni?" Scarlett asked Bria. "Is she freaking out?"

Bria scanned the audience for her teacher's face. "I don't see her."

"Oh my gosh, she was probably so embarrassed that she left!" Scarlett exclaimed. "That was the meanest thing I've ever seen. That was even mean for Justine."

"And that was just our first number," Mandy said, suddenly appearing behind them. "Wait till you see my duet with Phoebe." She wiggled her pointer finger in Liberty's face. "You are so going down."

Rochelle waited for Liberty to say something—anything—to zing Mandy back. But Liberty had nothing! Mandy skipped away, gloating.

"You're unbelievable!" Rochelle shouted at Liberty. "You insult me and everyone else on this team, and now—when we could actually use that big mouth to defend our team and Miss Toni, you zip it?"

"I agree with them," Liberty said. "Our costumes are lame; our dances are lame. I mean, come on, have you seen Bria and Anya's star dance?"

"Hey!" Anya piped up. "I know the costumes are ridiculous, but the dance is pretty good."

"Excuse me?" Bria shouted. "My mom and I

worked for hours on these costumes. They are not ridiculous."

"Maybe ridiculous is a strong word," Scarlett said, trying to calm them down. "Maybe what Anya meant to say is that they're a little loud."

"Loud?" Bria bristled. "You think my costumes are loud, Scarlett? I thought you were on my side."

"Look, your dance is no worse than our monkey routine," Rochelle offered.

"I like monkeys." Gracie tried to put her two cents in.

"Stay out of this, Grace Face," Liberty shot back.

"Hey, don't call my little sister that," Scarlett said, stepping between them.

"You do!" Liberty said. "On the bus this morning, you said she was an annoying baby."

Gracie's lower lip started to quiver. "I am not a baby!" She burst into tears.

"Gracie, cut it out," Scarlett said, frustrated. "If you don't want anyone to call you a baby, then don't act like one."

Just then, a voice boomed over the loudspeaker. "Next up in Junior Group Dance, Dance Divas with 'By the Beautiful Sea.' " The girls were too busy arguing to even hear their team being announced.

"Yoo-hoo," Mandy said, waving at them. She and her teammates were watching all the fireworks they'd caused. "I think that was your cue, Dance Dummies. Oopsies!"

Scarlett froze. "What? Did we just miss our entrance?"

"You did," said a stern voice. Miss Toni had come backstage to see what was holding up her team's performance. She looked furious. "Get out there this instant!" She tossed the beach ball at Rochelle.

The music was already playing and they were a beat behind and had to fight to catch up. Gracie was standing a foot too far to the left.

"What are you doing?" Scarlett said, grabbing on to the back of her bloomers and trying to pull her into line with the others.

Gracie tugged and Scarlett felt the fabric rip in her hands. The bloomers tore in half, and peeking out from under Gracie's costume was a pair of pink pig undies!

"Oh my gooshness!" Gracie yelped when she felt a draft and realized half of her costume was missing. She ran offstage in a hurry.

As the rest of the girls struggled to continue the dance, the ball soared over their heads. Each Diva was supposed to catch it midair and pass it on.

It was Scarlett's job to hold the ball as she did a side aerial. "Watch it, Anya!" She tried to warn her teammate as she accidentally kicked it out of her hands doing her *fouetté* turn.

"I got it!" Rochelle whispered as she did a graceful split and stretched forward to retrieve the ball. It rolled away from her fingertips and wound up under Bria's feet.

"Whoa!" Bria exclaimed, as she started her reverse leg hold turn. The ball rolled under her foot, and she lost her hold and toppled over. Still, she managed to pick it up and throw it at Liberty, who wasn't about to let anything detract from her *grand jeté*. Instead of catching it, she kicked the ball out of her way with all her might.

This time, the ball flew off the stage and bounced right off the lead judge's head. Scarlett couldn't look—not at the audience, not at the judges—as the Divas took their bows and walked back to the wings.

"That was a complete train wreck!" Rochelle said. "The audience was laughing at us."

Scarlett rubbed her temples. "There wasn't one thing that went right. Miss Toni is going to kill us."

"You're right about that," Toni said, glaring at them. "I have never been so humiliated in my life."

"Not even after City Feet made fun of you? 'Cause I thought that was more humiliating," Liberty pointed out.

"My own team, making a fool of me onstage

by botching the choreography, running offstage, falling on their butts, and assaulting a judge was much worse," their teacher said, scolding them. "I don't know what to do with you girls."

"We still have our duets," Bria said. "We'll do better, Miss Toni, we promise."

Toni didn't look convinced, but she didn't look angry anymore either. Just sad and tired. She went back to her seat in the audience.

"I think we really disappointed her." Scarlett sighed. "I feel bad." She turned to Liberty and Rochelle. "The only thing we can do is pull out a win in the Duets. We're counting on you guys." Their monkey routine was fourth up in the category, and they had only a few minutes to change into their costumes.

Rochelle nodded. "I'll do my best banana split," she said. "Get it? Split? That's dance humor."

Scarlett tried to smile but she had a sinking feeling the day's drama was far from over.

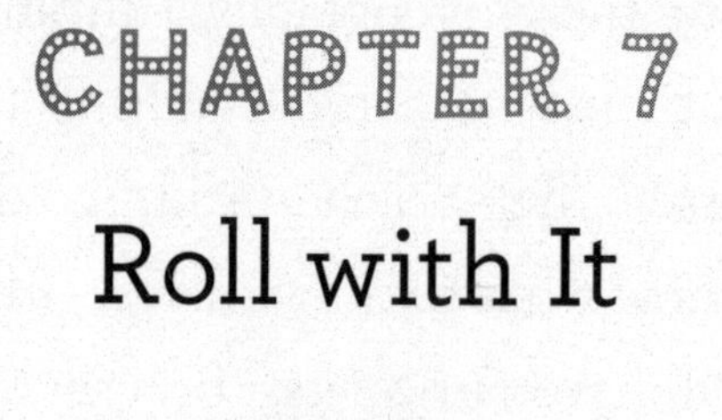

CHAPTER 7

Roll with It

"Just remember to keep the count," Rochelle reminded Liberty as they warmed up and waited their turn backstage. "One and roll and two and roll and three and . . ."

"Roll! I get it!" Liberty snapped. "Let's just get this over with it." She scratched at the fur on her monkey suit. "This thing smells like it's been in a litter box. *Eww.*"

"*Shhh,*" Scarlett hushed her. She pointed to Gracie, who was sniffling in the corner. "Let's cut the kitty talk, okay? Someone is really upset."

Liberty rolled her eyes. "I'm not the one who tore her costume, Big Sister Scoot."

"It was an accident," Scarlett insisted. "And I pinned it back so you can't see her undies anymore." But she doubted she could convince Gracie that the tear had been unintentional. Gracie refused to speak to Scarlett or even look in her direction. As far as Gracie was concerned, Scarlett did it on purpose to get even with her for ruining her leotard and tights. There was no convincing her otherwise.

"The first duo is up," Bria reported. "Sweet Peaches Dance Company from Marietta, Georgia. Their dance is called 'Lion Queens.'" She peeked out through the curtains and saw two girls dressed in fiery orange leotards with yellow sequins. One girl was swinging from a vine across the stage.

"Great," replied Rochelle, "more jungle acts. Just what we need to compete with our monkey routine."

"They're pretty fierce," Bria added, observing the duet's explosive acro moves. "One of them just did an amazing back layout with a half twist!"

Rochelle shook her head. "I can't watch. It's only making me more depressed."

"Next up," the announcer said into the microphone, "we have Explosion DC from Washington, DC, dancing a lyrical duet to 'Let It Go' from *Frozen*." Two girls emerged onstage wearing silver wigs and white dresses covered with dangling icicles. "You see that?" Bria pointed out to Anya. "*That's* a costume. You don't hear them complaining about too many icicles, do you?"

Anya watched the girls *pirouette* across the stage. "Are they supposed to be abominable snowmen . . . or porcupines? I can't tell," she replied.

"Nah, definitely chandeliers," Rochelle piped up. "But they are pretty good." She watched as one girl did a lively series of *chaînés* from one end of the stage to the other.

"Oh, I love this song!" Gracie clapped her hands. "It's from my favorite movie. But they need a snowman that talks."

"How about snow?" Scarlett asked. White snowflakes suddenly floated to the stage. The whole auditorium was a blizzard!

"Oh my gooshness!" Gracie squealed. "I wan
make a snow angel!"

Scarlett caught her just in time before she raced out in the middle of Explosion DC's duet. "Chill out, Gracie!" Scarlett reminded her. "It's not real snow, and it's not your duet!"

Gracie wrestled free of her grip. "You are the meanest sister in the world, Scoot!" she shouted, then stomped back to the dressing room.

"That was a close one," Bria whispered to Scarlett. "That Gracie is a handful. We could have been disqualified for sabotaging another team's routine."

"Tell me about it!" Scarlett sighed. "Sometimes Gracie just leaps before she looks."

The icicle-clad girls took their bows, then strutted past them. Rochelle peeked out to see the judges' reaction. "They seem a little icy," she reported to her fellow Divas. "That's good news for us."

The announcer stepped up to the microphone once again. "There will be a brief pause while we snowstorm," he said. "Then we will performing 'Rock and Roll.' "

goodie." Liberty smirked. "Stinky Feet get to follow the slushy sisters."

Mandy suddenly zipped by them on a pair of red sequined roller skates. "Make way, losers." She giggled.

"Seriously? A contemporary dance on wheels? Is that even allowed?" Anya asked.

"Oh yes, it's allowed," Regan said, watching her teammates take the stage. "It's never been done before—so I guess you could say we're making history here at Dance Fusion."

"Did you say history—or mystery? Because the judges look pretty confused as to why Mandy is spinning in circles like some circus act," Liberty said.

"Attagirl," Rochelle told her fellow Diva. "That's the loudmouth Liberty we know and love."

Regan looked out at the audience. They did seem a bit dizzy. The judges were also whispering among themselves. As Addison played an air guitar, Mandy continued whipping around the stage, faster and faster. “I don’t think she’s supposed to do that,” she said. “She’s going too fast.”

“Ya think?” Liberty said. “Maybe Mandy’s a little confused. She thinks this is a roller derby, not a dance competition.”

Suddenly, a little voice screamed from the stage. “Help! I can’t stop!”

Phoebe raced over to see what was going on. “OMG! I told Miss Justine this was a bad idea! That wood floor is really slippery after that snow number.”

Addison grabbed on to Mandy’s elbow, trying to anchor her. But she was going too fast.

“It’s Newton’s First Law of Motion,” Bria said, recalling the last physics test she had crammed for. “A body in motion stays in motion . . .”

“Until it goes splat!” Liberty smirked. “Which is what Mandy just did right in front of the judges.”

The Tiny Terror was lying on her back with

her feet in the air, wheels still spinning, moaning in agony.

"Ladies and gentlemen, we'll take a short break," the announcer's voice broke through the last chords of the music. "Can someone please call a medic?"

Mandy slowly got to her feet. "No, wait. I'm fine! The show must go on!" She smiled sweetly and winked at the judges. She did an elegant *arabesque* on her roller skates, then faced the crowd and curtsied. The audience applauded wildly and gave her a standing ovation.

"I'm going to be sick," Bria said in disbelief. "She just wiped out and they love her!"

"She wiped out on purpose," Rochelle said, gritting her teeth. "She's trying to get the sympathy vote."

"We wiped out a dozen times in our group routine. You think we'll get the sympathy vote?" Anya asked.

"No, because we didn't fake an injury. Look at her!" Liberty said. Addison was holding Mandy around the waist as she rolled her gently off the stage.

"Aw, Mandy go boom?" Liberty asked as she skated by, cradling her elbow.

"For your information, she's really hurt!" Addison said. She pointed to a small purple bruise on Mandy's elbow. "Can someone please get us an ice pack? A doctor?"

"An Academy Award for Best Actress?" Rochelle offered. " 'Cause that was the fakest fall I have ever seen."

Justine pushed past the Divas to check on Mandy. "Are you okay, sweetie?" she asked. "Does it hurt?"

Mandy nodded her head. "Uh-huh. Addison pulled it really hard."

"It was an accident," her teammate insisted. "I was trying to help you brake—not *break*—your arm."

"I'm sure the judges appreciate how you kept going, even in the face of a painful injury," Justine said. "That's what a professional does."

"And that's what a liar does," Liberty said, challenging her. "Did you see how she played those judges? Just so they'd feel bad for her?"

"I feel bad for you—for all of you," Justine said. "I think the whole Diva 'tude has gone to your heads. Yours, too." She motioned to Toni, who came to see what was going on.

"Roller skates? Really, Justine?" Toni smirked. "So predictable."

Rochelle elbowed Scarlett. "What does she mean?"

"Just like at ABC when Melissa Donovan threw her Sweet Sixteen party at RollerJam USA," Toni continued. "Remember?"

Scarlett shrugged. "She's lost me. Some ballet school drama from back in the day."

"She's lost me, too," Justine replied. "I have no idea what you're talking about, Toni."

"Really? You don't remember how you pretended to fall on your roller blades right in front of Marcus Sanzobar so he'd come to your rescue?"

"Now, Marcus I do remember—he dumped you for me." Justine smiled maliciously.

"You weren't hurt back then, and I seriously doubt Mandy is hurt now," Toni said. "At least, I hope not. Because if you purposely did anything to put one of your pupils at risk . . ."

Justine cut her off. "Nonsense! Mandy is an expert skater. The floor was just a little too slick. She'll be fine." She ushered Mandy back to the dressing rooms.

"Do you believe her?" Rochelle asked their coach.

Toni sighed. "It doesn't matter if I believe her or not. What matters is what the judges think. And there's nothing we can do about that, is there?"

She adjusted the yellow banana headdress on Rock. "I want it clean, precise, flawless. Clear?" she said.

"Clear!" Rochelle and Liberty replied.

Toni nodded. "Then get out there and show them what the Divas are made of."

CHAPTER 8

It's a Jungle out There

The sounds of wild animals filled the auditorium: lions, tigers, and monkeys, oh my! Liberty and Rochelle took their places on opposite sides of the stage. As the music began to play, Rochelle performed a series of split rolls while Liberty did a chest stand, kicking her feet high above her head.

"So far, so good," Anya commented. "They look great out there."

The next part of the duet was the hardest: Rock had to roll across the floor as Liberty "dove" over her. On the last dive, her monkey tail got caught in the zipper of her costume. As she and

Rock stood up to do their simultaneous *fouettés*, the tail was wrapped so tightly around her chest that she could barely move her legs. She looked like a monkey mummy.

She turned her back to the audience and tried to fix it. "I'm stuck," she whispered to Rochelle. "I can't move in this stupid costume!"

No matter how hard she tugged, the tail wouldn't come free. "Help me!" she said. Rochelle pulled on the tail while Liberty yanked on the zipper.

"What are they doing?" Bria asked. "Playing tug-of-war?"

All of a sudden, the tail released, and Rochelle fell backward, pulling Liberty down on top of her. "Get off of me!" she screamed. "You're ruining the dance!"

"I'm ruining it? Who just knocked me over?" Liberty shouted. They began wrestling on the floor, completely forgetting they were in the middle of Dance Fusion!

"Rock! No!" Scarlett called from the wings.

But it was too late. The music had stopped, and they were brawling on the floor. Liberty peeled all of Rock's bananas off her headpiece, and Rock tied her tail in a huge knot. Toni raced to the stage to break them up.

"Enough!" she barked, pulling them to their feet. Both costumes were in tatters. "Have you completely lost your minds?"

The girls stared out at the audience, who were staring right back at them.

She dragged them backstage, where normally she would have demanded they both turn in their Divas jackets had Justine and City Feet not been there listening to every word.

"We will discuss this later," Toni told them both.

Anya and Bria were up next, and they were her last hope. Anya squirmed in her leotard. It weighed a ton thanks to all of the intricate beading Bria and her mom had stitched on it.

"Light, delicate, ethereal," their teacher had instructed them.

The music was soft and twinkly—almost like a lullaby—and Bria and Anya twirled around the stage as if they were dancing on the clouds.

Gracie stopped moping long enough to sneak a peek. "Pretty," she said softly. "Magicificent."

Scarlett smiled. "Is that magic and magnificent rolled together?" she asked her little sister.

Gracie huffed. "What do you care? You're the meanest person in the whole world!" She went back to her corner.

"Oh boy." Scarlett sighed. "This has been some crazy competition."

Rochelle handed her a plastic banana—all that was left of her hat. "Yup, I'd say it was pretty bananas."

At least things were going well for Bria and Anya's duet. They just had a few more minutes to go. Anya waited patiently in fifth position as Bria leaped around the stage. Anya noticed a long string hanging from the strap of her leotard. *Oh no*, she thought. What if Miss Toni or the judges saw it? She quickly gave it a tug—then regretted it. All the beading on her bodice began to unravel.

The last part of the duet called for simultaneous *fouettés*—twenty-five of them in a row. As Anya began to spin, the shiny metal stars Bria had sewn on flew off her costume, pelting the judges in the face.

"Ow!" yelped one woman. She shielded her face with her papers, as if she was under attack.

Another judge got an eyeful. "I can't see!" he said squinting. "I think one of those things scratched my cornea!"

"Stop! Young lady, please!" the head judge begged Anya. "Your stars are a lethal weapon!"

Breathless, Anya stopped spinning. She looked down at her costume. Only a few stars remained on the blue velvet. "I told you," she whispered to Bria. "Now do you believe me? This costume is a menace!"

"I didn't tell you to pull it apart!" Bria fired back. "You're the menace!"

The announcer ushered them off the stage, where they continued fighting.

“You can never admit when you’re wrong,” Anya yelled. “Little Miss Perfect can’t say these costumes were a stupid idea!”

Bria fumed. “That is so not true. You’re just not a team player, Anya. You always have to have it your way.”

Toni did nothing this time to stop the fighting. She stood there silently, letting the girls go at each other. No one even noticed she was there until she cleared her throat.

“Oh my gosh, Miss Toni!” Scarlett said. “We’re sorry.”

“Are you?” Toni said quietly. “I don’t think so. I don’t think any of you are sorry for your behavior or your actions today. But I’m sorry. I’m sorry I ever invested my heart and time into a team that doesn’t care about each other.”

She walked back to the audience to await the awards ceremony. They all knew it wouldn’t be good news—there was no way any of their routines would come in first place. The only consolation prize would be if they had somehow managed to beat City Feet.

When it came time to announce the Junior Duets, Anya and Bria gave each other dirty looks, which was nothing compared to what Liberty and Rochelle did to each other. Scarlett had to sit between them just to keep them from pulling each other's hair.

"In fifth place, Dance Divas Studio with 'Going Bananas,'" the announcer read. Then he turned to the judges. "Are you sure?"

"You go get it," Liberty told Rock. "I'm too embarrassed."

"I will not!" Rochelle refused. "You go get it."

The judge finally walked over and handed the trophy to Scarlett. "Maybe you should hold on to this?" he said.

The Hippie Chicks took fourth place for their "Zombie Love" duet.

"Seriously?" Bria sighed. "They beat us with body parts falling off of them?"

The announcer took a deep breath before reading the third-place title holder. "I would like to assure the audience that Ms. Goldberg, our esteemed judge, will be just fine. She'll be wearing an eye patch for a little while, but . . ."

Anya growled at Bria. "Great job. We blinded a judge!"

"Nonetheless," the announcer continued, "our third-prize spot goes to 'Count the Stars,' Dance Divas Studio." Anya and Bria both stood up and gave each other a shove.

Second place went to two of the Groovy Boyz for their Super Bowl–inspired routine, "Touchdown." Which left only one team for first . . .

"Congratulations, 'Rock and Roll,' City Feet!" the announcer boomed. "What a comeback!"

Mandy bounced up to receive the trophy. Her left arm was in a sling, but she managed to blow kisses with her right one to the judges.

The group titles were just as disappointing. "By the Beautiful Sea" didn't even make the top ten. At least City Feet's Diva diss didn't win first place. They came in second behind the Fab 5 from Philly and their rendition of the Beatles' "Yesterday" performed as a tap routine.

"At least Miss Toni will be glad about that," Scarlett said. Their teacher was heading for them with a scowl on her face. "Or maybe not?"

"Everyone, in the dressing room, now!" Toni commanded. "This calls for drastic measures."

CHAPTER 9

Toni's Test

The Divas had no idea what Toni meant by "drastic measures," but they were pretty sure it wasn't going to be fun.

"You think she's going to kick us all off the team?" Bria asked Scarlett as they walked to the changing room.

Scarlett shrugged. "I don't know. I've never seen her this mad before."

When they opened the door, Toni was pacing the floor. "Sit," she said firmly. The girls all took seats on the floor.

"Does anyone know why we lost today?" she

began. She scanned the faces in the room, waiting for someone to volunteer an answer. Finally, Gracie's hand went up.

"'Cause some people were mean?" she said, glaring at Scarlett.

"Because everyone was mean to each other. Because no one here, not one of you, acted like you belonged on a team," Toni explained. "And I cannot have that."

Scarlett gulped. This was it. The Dance Divas Elite Competition Team was history. "Please, Miss Toni!" she pleaded. "Can't we have one more chance? We can show you that we are a great team."

Toni shook her head. "I don't believe that—not after what I saw today. And I won't believe it until you prove me wrong."

"How are we gonna do that?" Anya asked. "Dance Fusion is over."

"Precisely," Toni answered her. "There are no more chances for you to fix what happened here today. It's going to take more than dancing to convince me that any of you are worthy of calling yourselves Divas ever again."

Scarlett gulped. She knew Toni meant business. But if they couldn't dance to prove themselves worthy, then what?

"Tomorrow, I want all of you to meet me at the studio at seven a.m. sharp. Bring your mothers with you. I'll need them to sign a permission slip."

"Ooh, are we going on a class trip—like to the circus?" Gracie suggested. "That's when my teacher has us get permission slips."

"No, no circus," Toni answered. "But I will tell you this: where I'm taking you will require you to work as a team. If not, you won't survive."

"Survive?" Liberty spoke up. "My mother will never agree to anything that's dangerous . . . or icky."

"Actually, since your mother is still in Hollywood, I sent her an e-mail," Toni replied. "And she was one hundred percent in favor of my idea. She thinks it will be good for you to get your hands dirty."

Liberty looked panic-stricken. "But I just got a manicure!"

"Get our hands dirty? What's she gonna make us do?" Rochelle whispered to her teammates. "Plant rosebushes behind the studio? Haul garbage to the dump? Wash her car?"

"I bet she'll have us clean out that dusty old prop closet at the studio," Bria said. "Who knows what's living in there . . ."

"No more talking," Toni hushed them. "If you want to remain a Diva, you will be at the studio tomorrow morning. And leave your dance bags at home."

* * *

Back at home that night, Scarlett told her mom exactly what Toni had said.

"I can't say I blame her," her mom replied. "It drives me crazy when you two fight over silly things."

Scarlett glanced over at Gracie, who was trying to tie a small silver bell around their kitten's neck while he wiggled out of it.

"I'm going to start dinner. Play nice," their mom warned them.

Scarlett rolled her eyes. She was too old to play any of her little sister's crazy games. And the one she was working on at the moment looked particularly bizarre. Gracie was arranging a bunch of boxes, cans, and assorted toys all around the living room.

"What are you doing?" she asked, then instantly regretted it. Gracie took it as an invitation to join in.

"Oh! It's the Kitten Olympics. See, this is Mr. Mustard's obstacle course. And if he completes it, he wins a solid-gold medal," Gracie explained.

"Really? Where are you going to get a solid-gold medal?" Scarlett asked.

Gracie scratched her head. She hadn't thought about that. "Can I borrow one of your dance ones?" she asked.

Scarlett's face turned brick red. "No way! You do not touch any of my dance medals, do you hear me? They're special, and they're mine!"

But Gracie was already on her feet, racing up the stairs to Scarlett's bedroom.

"Did you hear me, Gracie?" Scarlett shouted after her. "I said NO!"

"Just one? I'll borrow it and give it back. Promise!" Gracie called down.

Scarlett bounded up the stairs after her. "This is the last straw, Gracie. I mean it! If you take one more of my things, I am going to put a lock on my room to keep you out. Or better yet: I'll put a lock on your room to keep you in!"

She found her little sister standing on her bed, examining a dozen or so of Scarlett's medals hanging off of a hook in the wall over her headboard.

"Come down now," Scarlett fumed. "Touch one thing and that's it . . ."

Gracie smiled. "You mean like this, Scoot?" She unhooked a medal and slipped it over her head. "I think it looks really good on me."

Scarlett gritted her teeth. "Give. It. Back." As she lunged for her, Gracie bounced off the bed like it was a trampoline. She dangled the medal in front of her. "Catch me! Catch me! You can't catch me!"

This time, Scarlett aimed low—she grabbed Gracie around the ankles and wouldn't let go. "Hand it over!"

Gracie tried to wiggle away. She looked like a penguin. "Cut it out!" she screamed. "Mommy! Scarlett won't let me have one of her stupid gold medals for Mr. Mustard!"

Suddenly, they both froze in their tracks. Where was Mr. Mustard?

"You left the kitty downstairs by himself?" Gracie asked. "He's a baby! He'll get hurt!"

Scarlett immediately released her grip. "I'm sure he's fine." But she was just as worried.

They raced down the steps and looked in the living room. There was no cat in sight. "Yoo-hoo, Mr. Mustard," Gracie called. "Come out, come out wherever you are."

Scarlett peered under the couch, behind the window curtains, and even inside their mom's favorite vase on the coffee table. No Mr. Mustard.

"Where could he be?" Gracie asked anxiously.

Then they heard a tinkling-bell sound coming from down the hallway.

"Mr. Mustard!" they both cried. They ran into the foyer to find the tiny kitten on the very tip-top of their mom's china cabinet.

"Oh my gooshness!" Gracie exclaimed. "How did he get all the way up there? I can't even reach up there!"

"He must be a good climber," Scarlett said. "We have to get him down."

She pulled out a step stool from the closet. "Here, kitty, kitty," she sang. "Come on down, kitty, kitty."

Their mom heard all the commotion and came out to investigate. "What are you two doing?"

"Mr. Mustard is in trouble, Mommy," Gracie said, flinging her arms around her mother's waist. Her eyes were brimming with tears. "We have to save him!"

"I think I can almost reach him," Scarlett said, stretching on her tiptoes. But when she touched his tail, the kitten backed farther away.

"Ugh," Scarlett said, sighing. "It's no use."

"But we have to rescue him!"

"It's times like this I wish your dad was still here," their mother said. "He's six feet tall."

"Call Daddy! Call the fire department! Call anyone!" Gracie pleaded. "What if he jumps!"

Scarlett got down off the stool and put her arm around Gracie. "Look, I know you're scared, but we can't panic. We have to think." She noticed Mr. Mustard's favorite toy—a purple pom-pom ball—in the corner of the stairs. "I think I have an idea—but I need your help, Gracie. Go get one of your dolls and some yarn."

Gracie returned and Scarlett took the Barbie from her, posing it so the arms were stretched high over her head. She tied a piece of yarn to one of the doll's hands and the other to the ball. "You hold this and climb up on my shoulders—just like you did in the "Leaning Tower of Pisa" dance we did for Dance Starz America," she instructed her sister. Gracie obeyed, and Scarlett held tight to the backs of her legs and ankles.

"Careful girls," their mother said nervously. "I can't look!"

Together, Scarlett and Gracie were tall enough to reach the top of the cabinet. "Now wiggle the doll at Mr. Mustard," Scarlett said. "Make it a game."

"Hello, little kitty," Gracie said in a high-pitched voice. "Look what I got for you!"

The kitten was curious and came closer. "Gotcha!" Gracie shouted, grabbing the kitten in her other hand. Scarlett gently lowered them both down to the floor.

"Oh, Mr. Mustard, you scared us!" Gracie said, cuddling him. "Don't you ever do that again!"

"How did he get all the way up there?" her mother asked. "It must be seven feet high!"

"Obviously, he takes after Gracie," Scarlett said. "He has amazing acro moves!" She suddenly remembered what their fight had been about. It seemed so silly now—especially when their kitten had almost been hurt because of it.

She ran upstairs and got one of her gold dance medals and brought it down to Gracie. "Here," she said. "That was a gold-medal rescue if I ever saw one."

"Really?" Gracie smiled. "I can keep it?"

"Yeah," Scarlett said, shrugging. "I have plenty of other ones. You can have it to play Kitten Olympics."

"Will you play it with me?" Gracie asked, hopefully. She handed the kitten to Scarlett. "Mr. Mustard says, 'Pretty please, Scoot?' "

Scarlett chuckled. How could she say no to both Gracie's begging *and* the kitten's purring? "Okay, you win. Get the obstacle course ready!"

Gracie was delighted and ran back to the living room to finish arranging the "Bobcat Bobsled."

She hoped that ending her feud with Gracie would be a step in the right direction toward making peace among all the Divas tomorrow. But she doubted it would be as easy.

CHAPTER 10

Ready to Rough It

Miss Toni tossed out a khaki-colored backpack in the middle of the studio floor. "Do you know what this is?" she asked.

"A bad example of how to accessorize?" Liberty joked.

"It's a camping backpack. You're all going camping tomorrow as soon as we get you suited up for it. I know it's a Monday, but you all have the day off from school while your teachers have an in-service day."

Bria raised her hand. "Camping? You mean like sleeping in the woods, where there are bugs and snakes and wild animals?"

"And Bigfoot!" Gracie chimed in.

"Then you'll all just have to stick together to survive, won't you?" their coach replied. "I've spoken with all your parents and they approve—although, Bria, your mother insists you study for your science test. I told her I'd make sure you bring a flashlight with extra batteries."

"Great," Bria groaned. "Can hardly wait."

"I don't actually own any camping stuff," Rochelle spoke up. "I don't do camping."

"Well, you do now. I gave your mothers a list and sent them off shopping. You'll need canteens, hiking boots, sleeping bags . . ." She handed Scarlett a map. "You're in charge of navigating."

Scarlett read the name on the map. "Black Boulder Forest? Is that place dangerous?"

"Only if you don't work as a team," Toni said. "We leave bright and early tomorrow morning. You'll have to hike on a trail, set up your campsite, build a fire, and rustle up some grub. *All* before the sun sets."

"Grub?" Liberty groaned. "What kind of grub? Can't I call my mom and have it catered?"

"No catering, no moms, no assistance whatsoever," Toni dictated. "This is exactly what you girls need."

"To starve to death or be killed by grizzly bears?" Liberty shrieked.

"No, a wake-up call. A dose of reality. You'll be hiking several miles to the site. A park ranger and I will follow close behind, but there'll be no help unless it's an emergency."

Rochelle laughed. "Liberty breaking a nail is an emergency."

Bria looked nervous. She'd never "roughed it" before. "What if we don't want to go?" she asked.

"Then you certainly don't have to. I won't force you," Toni said. "You can just hand in your Dance Divas jacket and find another studio to dance at."

She turned and walked out the door, leaving the girls behind to discuss her proposition.

"So we have no choice," Anya said. "We have to go on Toni's camping trip or get kicked off the team."

Scarlett flipped through the forest guide. It looked huge, with lots of hills, trails, and lakes. "Maybe it will be fun," she suggested. "A Divas' adventure."

"Did you see *The Hunger Games?*" Liberty asked her.

"If we have to go, then we should try and make the best of it," Scarlett insisted. "It's only one night. We're tough. We can do it."

She raised her hand in the air for a Divas' cheer: *"Divas rock, divas roll! Divas are always in control!"* None of the others joined in—except for Bria, who had her own lyric to add:

"Divas alone in the woods? None of this sounds very good!"

CHAPTER 11

Camp Diva

When a van pulled up in front of the studio the next day at 6:00 a.m., none of the girls were excited—and they were barely awake.

"This is barbaric," Liberty said, yawning. "Who ever heard of packing a backpack? All my luggage has wheels." She struggled to hoist the sack over her shoulders and make her way over to where the rest of the Divas were waiting.

"Toni said to pack light," Rochelle pointed out. "What do you have in there?"

"Just the bare necessities," Liberty replied. "Pedicure kit, moisturizer, cordless curling iron, cell phone charger, cashmere blanket—oh, and my lamb Pillow Pet of course!"

Rochelle rolled her eyes. "How about some canned food and water?"

"Nope, but I do have several issues of *Teen Vogue* for when we get bored!"

"I brought a compass," Anya volunteered. She held up a tarnished silver disk on a chain. "My dad said it belonged to my great grandpa Alexei in Russia. It's kinda my good-luck charm whenever I travel, but it might actually come in handy this time."

"Who needs a compass when I have this?" Bria held up her phone and pointed to her GPS app. "I can find anywhere on the planet with this."

"Assuming you can get a cell phone signal in the woods," Rochelle reminded her. "I wouldn't count on Wi-Fi wherever Toni is taking us."

"Or a bathroom," Scarlett said. "I don't think there's such a thing as a ladies' room in the wild."

Liberty wrinkled her nose. "That is so disgusting! How am I supposed to do my nighttime beauty ritual without a sink?"

Rochelle shook her head. "You're worrying about your beauty? I'm worried about my life! What if there are ferocious beasts out there? I don't want to be some grizzly bear's midnight snack!"

Scarlett tried to keep them all calm. There was no use in freaking out . . . yet. "I'm sure Miss Toni wouldn't put us in any danger," she said. "She's our teacher, after all." She saw her dance coach loading up the van with assorted camping gear and hoped there was an air mattress in there as well.

"I hope she got me a pink sleeping bag," Gracie commented. "Pink is my fave color, though purple would be okay, I guess." Her backpack was filled with stuffed animals: Petunia Pig, Gerdie Gorilla, and her latest addition: a red cat she named Ketchup Kitty.

"You couldn't leavc a few of those at home?" Rochelle asked her.

Gracie shook her head. "Nuh-uh. I need them to keep me snuggly at night."

Scarlett had already been through this discussion at 5:00 a.m. When Gracie's canteen, change of clothes, and warm socks wouldn't fit in her bag, her mom handed them to Scarlett to carry in hers.

"But Mom," Scarlett had whined. "I have my own stuff to take."

"You are the big sister, so you have to look out for Gracie," she warned her. Gracie then presented her with Tessie Teddy Bear. "You can carry her for me," she said. "Thanks, Scoot."

"Let's face it. We're all clueless." Bria sighed. She was going through a checklist her mother had prepared for her. "I think I forgot to pack a toothbrush."

"I'm not clueless," Anya spoke up. She was checking to make sure her canteen was filled with water. "I went camping once when I lived in California."

"Really?" Liberty raised an eyebrow. "Your backyard doesn't count."

"It wasn't my backyard," Anya defended herself. "It was in a state park with my Brownies troop."

"Brownies? How old were you?" Rochelle asked.

"Seven or eight. I know it had to be in second grade . . ."

Bria chuckled. "Oh, great. That makes me feel so much better!"

"It doesn't matter," Scarlett said, trying to keep everyone calm. They hadn't even left on the trip yet, and they were already bickering! "We'll learn as we go along."

"Miss Toni says she wants us to learn an important lesson," Gracie reminded them.

"Yeah," Bria said. "I just hope that lesson doesn't involve a pack of wild werewolves."

"You've seen one too many movies." Rochelle chuckled. "Come on? Werewolves? Bloodthirsty coyotes, sure. Maybe poisonous snakes. But no werewolves."

"Snakes?" Liberty gulped. "I don't like snakes . . . at all." She unzipped her bag and pulled out a can of bug repellent. "Do you think this keeps away snakes, too?"

Gracie held up her stuffed animal. "Miss Petunia Pig will protect us," she said. "She's very brave."

Scarlett seriously doubted a tattered pink pig with a missing ear would help them fend off wild animals, but it was a nice thought.

"Okay, everyone on board," Toni said. She glanced down at Liberty's pink sequined sneakers. "Really? That's what you're hiking through mud and rough terrain in? I thought I told you to wear hiking boots."

"The hiking boots my mom bought me were hideous," Liberty sniffed. "I don't do ugly footwear." She pulled up her leggings to reveal socks with pink stars on them. "There's no reason why camping has to be unfashionable."

* * *

The campsite was two hours away. The roads were long and twisty and seemed to climb higher and higher into the hills. The sun rose above the trees in a red ball.

"Are we going up a mountain?" Bria asked, peering out the window.

"Would you prefer to hike up or down?" Toni asked. "I thought I was being nice by making it easier on you. You'll hike down to the site."

"If she wanted to make it easier on us, she could have just taken us shopping at the mall," Liberty muttered under her breath.

When they arrived, a park ranger was waiting to greet them. "Ladies—or should I say Divas—welcome to Black Boulder Forest! I'm Ranger Sam and I'm at your service." He sounded so enthusiastic, like this would be the best trip of their lives. But no one was buying it.

"Can you please show us to our accommodations?" Liberty said, dragging her backpack behind her. "I could really use a nice shower and spa treatment right now. Where's the hotel?"

The ranger laughed. "I'm sorry, but your only accommodations are the tents you'll set up when you make your way to the bottom of the mountain."

Miss Toni held up a vinyl duffel. "Got 'em right here! I hope they'll be to your liking, Liberty. I rented the top-of-the-line model with high-wind protection."

"That's great!" Ranger Sam replied. "It can get very cold out there at night. You're in for a treat."

Scarlett glanced over at Liberty. She looked like she was going to keel over. "What? No hotel? Not even a villa or cabana or *something*?" she exclaimed.

"Where are the beds?" Scarlett asked. "There are beds to sleep in, aren't there?"

Miss Toni smiled brightly. "Of course there are! I got each and every one of you your very own comfy sleeping bag." She tossed a green sack at Liberty. "Catch!"

Then she handed a lantern to Scarlett, a bag filled with pots and pans to Rochelle, and two totes stocked with food to Bria and Gracie.

"I highly recommend the powdered hummus and the dehydrated sweet potatoes," she said. "Yum!"

"What about breakfast?" Gracie piped up. It was her favorite meal of the day, and she couldn't imagine it without a heaping pile of pancakes or her mom's apple-cinnamon oatmeal.

"Glad you asked!" Toni replied. She handed her a dry box of bran cereal. "Help yourself. There's no milk, of course."

Bria rifled through the bag. There was absolutely nothing appetizing and her stomach was growling. "Maybe we can make a campfire and roast some s'mores," she suggested.

"That would be nice," Toni answered, "if you had any marshmallows and knew how to light a fire by rubbing two sticks together. Good luck with that!" She walked over to Ranger Sam. "You guys should definitely hit the trail right away. It'll take you several hours to reach the bottom, and you don't want to lose the daylight."

Bria gulped. "You mean, we'll have to walk

through the woods in the dark?" She tugged on Rochelle's sleeve and whispered, "Werewolves!"

Scarlett held up her lantern. "I guess that's why we have this." She looked at Miss Toni. "What happens if we get lost or in trouble?"

Ranger Sam handed her a whistle. "We won't be far behind, and I'll be keeping an eye on you. But you girls are leading *us*, not the other way around." He held up a pair of binoculars. "If you get into a bind, just toot for help."

Toni crossed her arms over her chest. She was not about to change her mind and let them all just go home. "Tick tock," she said. "Time to hit the trail."

CHAPTER 12

Not-So-Happy Trails

Scarlett looked around, trying to get her bearings and figure out where they were on the map. "You'd think they would have marked it with an 'X' . . . ," she said. "You think we're here?" She held up the map so Rochelle could see it.

"Your guess is as good as mine," Rochelle replied.

"Let me see," Liberty said as she pulled it out of Scarlett's hands.

"Why? You think you're Dora the Explorer?" Rock teased.

"No, but I can find my way expertly around the Riverside Square Mall floor plan. This can't be much harder." She pointed to a spot at the top of the map. "Here. This is where we are."

Scarlett shrugged. "Okay. I'll buy that. We're clearly way up high and the campsite is way down low."

"I want to snap a picture of us to post on Instagram!" Bria said, digging her phone out of her pocket.

"Great. Take a picture before we're eaten alive by wild animals," Anya said.

"Don't say that!" Bria hushed her. "Seriously! The wild animals might hear you. Don't give them any ideas!"

Liberty struck a pose. "Okay, everyone behind me and say cheese."

Rochelle frowned. "Behind you? Why do you get to be front and center?" She gave her teammate a shove so she could stand next to her. "Scarlett, over here next to me."

Bria rested her phone on a rock and set the auto-timer. "Okay, everyone get in. On the count of three, say 'DIVAS!' ONE TWO THREE . . ."

The flash went off before they could open their mouths.

Bria looked at the picture. The only person you could see was Gracie. Everyone else was cut off at the shoulders.

"I guess we have to scooch down to Gracie's height," Bria suggested.

"Scooch? You want me to scooch in my designer jeans?" Liberty groaned. "I am not getting all filthy so you can get a photo."

"Aw, come on," Rochelle taunted her. "You're not afraid of a little dirt, are ya?" She took a handful of soil and rubbed it into Liberty's studded leather jacket. "Oops! Looks like you'll have to send this to the dry cleaners!"

Liberty's face got bright red. "Do you have any idea how expensive this jacket is?" she screamed.

"Nope, but I'm sure you're gonna tell me," Rochelle replied.

"It's one-of-a-kind! It was a gift from Gaga!"

"Gaga gave you a jacket?" Bria gasped.

"No. She gave it to my mom and I kind of borrowed it from her closet . . . She's gonna kill me!"

Anya giggled. "It's a Gaga-tastrophe."

"It isn't funny," Liberty said, trying desperately to rub the stains out. "None of you are funny."

"I'm funny," Gracie piped up. "You wanna hear a joke?" She didn't wait for Liberty's answer. "Why did the lion lose at Monopoly? Because he was playing with a cheetah!" She cracked herself up. "Get it? A cheet-ah?"

"I still need a photo for Instagram," Bria reminded them. "Can we all just maybe sit over there on those rocks?" She pointed to a spot a few feet away. "Look, there's even a pretty backdrop."

Rochelle looked over. "Pretty backdrop? All I see are trees, trees, and more trees."

"Exactly," Bria said, pushing her into position. "It's very rustic."

"THREE TWO ONE . . . SAY 'DIVA!' "

This time when the camera flashed, they were all in the photo—but none of them were smiling and Gracie blinked.

"I give up," Bria said, sighing.

"This isn't a photo shoot. It's a do-or-die challenge," Anya reminded her.

"I think we should stop posing and get moving," Scarlett said, taking the map up again. "There'll be plenty of time for pics once we make our way down."

"Toni's totally enjoying torturing us," Liberty grumped. She could barely walk with the backpack over her shoulders and the bulky sleeping bag duffel in her arms.

Scarlett led the way, clutching the map, and tentatively making her way down the steep path. "This map has so many trails. I don't know which one to choose," she said.

Liberty peered over her shoulder. "Choose a short one. One that goes straight down and gets us out of here."

"There aren't any straight ones." Scarlett sighed.

"And they all have these weird names. Like Sleeping Bear Dunes and Biscuit Basin."

Gracie still had breakfast on the brain. "Go for the biscuit one. Maybe there's a pancake house on the way."

Scarlett studied the map from every angle. "I think we should take the Full Moon Trail," she said. "It winds around a big lake at the bottom, so we can wash up there, and it looks like there are some little rest stops along the way." She pointed to several brown triangles dotting the path.

Anya looked closely at the key. "Those aren't rest stops. They're bird-watching points. The only reason to stop there is if you want to get a look at the yellow-bellied sapsucker!"

"Oh," Scarlett replied. It had been a good guess.

"I think we should take this one. It seems the shortest," Bria suggested. She pointed to a curvy black line labeled 'OVERLOOK TRAIL.'

"As if I'd ever trust you—with trails or with costumes," Anya said.

"Guys, come on," Scarlett pleaded. "We have to make a decision, and Bria's path is just as good as any." She pointed to the left. "We go that way."

The path at the beginning of the trail was steep and narrow. "How are we supposed to walk on this and not break our necks?" Rochelle asked.

"Tippy-toes," Gracie suggested. She rose up in her hiking books on *relevé*.

"She means like we do in pointe class—and it's a great idea!" Scarlett said, taking tiny, quick, even steps down the path. "Everyone, *pas de bourrée*, one foot in front of the other." The girls formed a single, straight line and made their way down about twenty feet.

"Nice job," Scarlett said when they got to a more open area of the trail. She pointed to the map. "Now we can take a shortcut across this little trickling stream." But when they arrived at the spot, it was bigger and wetter than anticipated.

"That's no trickle!" Liberty exclaimed. "My shirt is one hundred percent silk, and I am not getting it soaking wet and ruined."

"It's so hard to tell from the map," Scarlett apologized. "I guess we could go back . . ."

"No, that's a huge waste of time," Anya said. "There's a stone path through the stream. We just have to skip between the stones."

Bria looked across the water. "That is no hop, skip, and jump. Those stones are really far apart."

"Bri, you have an amazing *grand jeté.* You can do it!" Scarlett cheered her on. "We all can."

She demonstrated by leaping from the shore to the first flat stone in the middle of the stream. "See? As Gracie would say, 'Easy-peasy!' "

"Easy-peasy for you to say," Rochelle groaned. "Okay. Everybody *jeté*! And make it as grand as you can."

They each followed behind Scarlett, leaping gracefully from stone to stone. Gracie wobbled on the last one, but Scarlett caught her arm and pulled her ashore.

"Good job," she told her little sister. "You're as good a leaper as Mr. Mustard."

Gracie smiled. "Ya think?"

"I think we're all in trouble," Bria said, studying the map over Scarlett's shoulder. "Does that say what I think it says? Did you just lead us to Nowhere Man's Path?"

Scarlett squinted at the tiny print. The trail they were standing on did have a pretty ominous name. "Well, lucky for us we're not men—we're Divas," she said. "Onward!"

CHAPTER 13

Carried Away

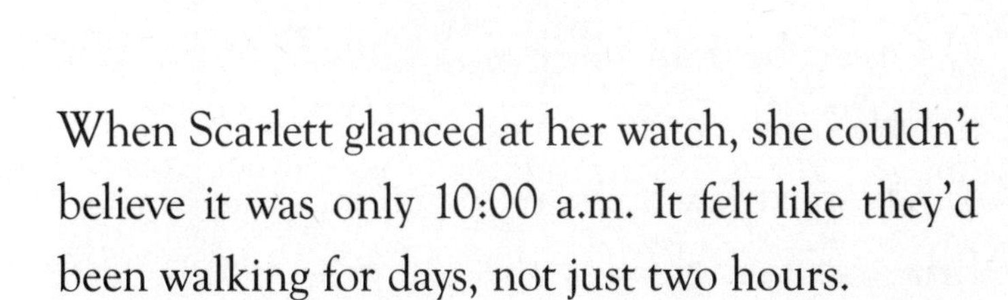

When Scarlett glanced at her watch, she couldn't believe it was only 10:00 a.m. It felt like they'd been walking for days, not just two hours.

"I'm starving," Anya said, sitting down on a rock to rest her aching feet. "Gracie, give me some of that cereal." Gracie shook the box; it was empty.

"You ate it *all*?" Liberty exclaimed. "That was supposed to be for all of us to share!"

"I couldn't help it," Gracie replied. "I was really hungry."

Scarlett took the tote of food out of her hands. "I'm sure there's a lot of other stuff in here." She pulled out a crumpled granola-bar wrapper, a near empty sports drink, and a bag of pretzels that had only crumbs left. "Gracie, how much did you eat?"

Her little sister shrugged. "I dunno. You can have these." She handed Anya a bag of freeze-dried green beans.

"*Eww!*" Anya said. "How am I supposed to eat this?"

Gracie held up a bean and smiled. "With your mouth?"

The next few hours didn't go much smoother. Bria was being eaten alive by mosquitoes, and Rochelle's hay fever was acting up.

"My eyes are so itchy I can barely see," she said. She sneezed into the sleeve of her hoodie.

"Gross!" Liberty pushed past her. "Keep your boogers to yourself."

"I can't help it," Rochelle said. "I'm allergic to something." She bent over to examine the tiny yellow flowers lining their path. "Maybe it's these guys." One whiff sent her into a sneezing fit.

"Hey! Quit it!" Liberty yelled. But Rochelle couldn't stop. Her last sneeze sent her colliding into Liberty, who bumped into a tree, then slipped and fell. When she looked down, there was a huge gash in one of the knees of her leggings.

"Oh my gosh! I'm bleeding!" Liberty screamed. Her knee was scraped and covered with dirt and gravel. "Ow, it hurts! It really hurts!"

Scarlett kneeled over her. "It doesn't look too bad. We just need to clean it. Someone hand me a canteen of water." Anya obliged, and they flushed out the wound. "We need to cover it with something. Anyone have a Band-Aid?"

Rochelle held up a clean tissue. "This is all I've got. Any idea how we can hold it in place?"

"Silly Putty!" Gracie suggested. "If I had any with me . . ."

"There's a roll of pink leopard-print duct tape in my backpack," Liberty said, choking back tears.

"Really? You didn't bring a first-aid kit but you brought duct tape?" Rock asked in disbelief.

"I thought if I got bored, I would make a cool

bracelet or a headband," she answered. "Insta-glamour."

It turned out it was also insta–first aid. Scarlett secured the tissue over the wound with the tape. It matched Liberty's pink sneakers. "I think it'll stay put for a while," Scarlett said. "Can you stand on it?" She helped Liberty to her feet.

"Ow!" she yelped. "It hurts! I don't think I can walk."

Rochelle couldn't take much more. "You are such a drama queen! It's barely a scrape."

"You did this!" Liberty fired back. "Your stupid sneeze knocked me down."

"And your ridiculous sneakers slipped on the gravel! Why couldn't you wear hiking boots like the rest of us?"

Scarlett blew her whistle in the air. Ranger Sam had told her to use it in an emergency, and this seemed like a good enough one. The girls were fighting, and Liberty was injured. She waited for him and Toni to race in and rescue them.

"Where are they?" Liberty moaned. "I'm dying and no one cares."

Bria laughed. "You are not dying. You just have a little boo-boo. Get over it."

"That's easy for you to say," Liberty pointed out. "You're not the one who's hurt."

They waited and whistled but still no one came. Scarlett had to do something. There was no one coming to their aid, and this arguing was getting them nowhere. "Rock, remember how you felt when you hurt your ankle and had to be on crutches?" she asked. "Maybe Liberty's really hurt. Maybe it's serious." She pointed to Liberty who was now in tears and cradling her bandaged knee.

Rochelle pouted. "Fine. Lean on me," she said. She offered her arm to Liberty, who looked positively horrified. "Come on. Do you want to stay here all day?"

"I don't think I can put pressure on my leg," Liberty said through gritted teeth. "I think you'll have to carry me."

Rochelle's eyes grew wide. "Carry you? Are you nuts? There is no way I'm gonna carry you!"

"We'll all take turns," Scarlett volunteered. "We can make a chair with our arms and carry Liberty down the mountain."

"Ooh! Can I get carried, too?" Gracie asked. "That sounds fun."

Rochelle rolled her eyes. "Fine." She linked arms with Scarlett, and Liberty sat between them. "This is the worst day of my life," she said as they struggled to make their way with their teammate in tow. She sneezed again, this time in Liberty's hair.

"*Eww!* Cut it out!" Liberty screamed.

"Would you like me to cover my nose and drop you?" Rochelle asked her. "'Cause that's my only option."

Liberty made a face. "This is the worst day of *my* life! A bloody knee *and* a shower of boogers."

Three hours later, they were nearly at the bottom of the trail. "It says to bear to the right," Bria pointed out. "Past Chickasaw Cave."

"Did you say chicken and slaw?" Anya asked.

Bria shook her head. "I said Chickasaw. It's an old Native American tribal name. Not a KFC!"

"Oh." Anya sighed. "I'm so hungry, I'm hearing things. I think I'm delirious."

Liberty dug into her purse and pulled out a box of Belgian chocolates. "Here. Have one," she said.

"OMG! You have truffles in your purse and you didn't say anything?" Anya grabbed them out of her hand and began stuffing them in her mouth.

"I forgot," Liberty explained. "I was a little busy bleeding."

"This is heaven," Anya said, licking her fingers. "Liberty, I never thought I'd say this, but I love you!"

"Hey, save some for me!" Gracie said, trying to wrestle one away from her.

"Are you kidding? You ate everything in our food bags! You were as piggy as your pink piggy, Gracie!" Anya held the box of chocolates high above her head so she couldn't reach it.

Gracie's eyes welled up. *Oh, no,* Scarlett thought. *Here we go . . .*

Anya saw the look on the little girl's face and stopped herself from popping the last one in her mouth. "I'm sorry, Gracie. Here, you can have one. Please don't cry!" She handed her a dark-chocolate candy with a hazelnut-cream center.

Gracie gobbled it down and smiled. "Thank you. That was yumilicious."

Scarlett was too busy trying to figure out the map to think of food. "I'm not sure what this little red leaf symbol here means," she said, showing it to Bria. "It's not anywhere on the key."

Bria shrugged. "Well, it's pretty. It must be those pretty red leaves over there." She pointed to a patch growing around the base of a tree. "Maybe I'll pick one for my scrapbook at home."

She was bending over a leaf when Anya suddenly screamed "*Noooooooo!*" and tackled her to the ground. Bria landed facedown in a pile of leaves and mud with Anya on top of her.

"Get off!" Bria said, spitting out a mouthful

of dirt. "Just because I made costumes you didn't like doesn't mean you have to beat me up!"

"No, I wasn't trying to beat you up," Anya said, helping Bria to her feet. "I was trying to save you from getting poison ivy. I remember it from my Girl Scouts guidebook."

"Poison ivy?" Bria gasped. "As in the stuff that makes you all itchy and rashy?"

Anya nodded. "You're welcome."

"Oh, so that's what the red leaf on the map meant," Scarlett said, making a note with a black pen on the side of the paper. "These map drawings could be a little better."

"Our map reader could be a lot better," Liberty said.

"Do you want to give it a try?" Scarlett said, throwing the map at her feet. "Honestly, I have had enough of everyone complaining and blaming me!"

Rochelle placed a hand on Scarlett's shoulder. "If you lose it, we will all lose it," she reminded her. "Scarlett, you're our leader. We need you to lead." She picked up the map and handed it to her.

"I'm just so tired," Scarlett moaned. "And it's getting darker."

"Then let's get where we're going," Rochelle said. "Anya and Bria, you're on ambulance duty." She pointed to Liberty. "If she talks too much, just drop her."

"Not funny," Liberty said through gritted teeth. "I am injured. Can we show some respect?"

"Let's all show some respect for each other," Scarlett said, picking up her bag and resuming the walk down the trail. "It's the only way we're going to get out of this mess."

CHAPTER 14

A Bewitching Tale

By the time they reached the bottom of the trail and settled on a spot to set up camp, it was nearly dusk. Carrying Liberty had definitely slowed them down.

"We better move fast before we lose the light," Scarlett instructed them. She opened the tent bag and looked inside. It was a mess of poles, hinges, and fabric pieces. "Does it come with an instruction booklet?" she asked, scratching her head.

"Let me Google 'How to build a tent,'" Bria suggested. But her phone had no service, not even when she held it up above her head. "I can't get a single bar," she said, shaking her phone. "It must be all those trees getting in the way."

"Any other suggestions?" Scarlett sighed. "We gotta get this thing up."

Gracie kneeled over the parts on the ground. "It's just like my Barbie tent," she said. "The one I set up in the backyard and decorated with your hair bows, Scoot." She suddenly remembered that she hadn't exactly mentioned borrowing her sister's hair accessories for decor. "Oops! Sorry!"

Scarlett didn't even care about the bows at the moment. She was exhausted, and just wanted a place for them all to sleep tonight. "Do you think you can figure it out?"

Gracie studied the pieces and sat down to work. She clicked one pole into another, then poked it through the hem in the bottom of the fabric. In less than an hour, she'd put the entire thing together by herself. She zipped the front door closed and stood back to admire her handiwork.

"Easy-peasy," she said, dusting off her hands. "It's not as pretty as my Barbie tent, but it works."

"Gracie, you never cease to amaze!" Scarlett said, hugging her little sister. "Great job."

They unrolled all the sleeping bags outside the tent, and piled a bunch of logs in the center of a circle to start a campfire.

"I think I saw this in a movie once," Bria said, rubbing two sticks together. But no matter how hard she rubbed, there was no spark—only a few pitiful puffs of smoke. The logs refused to catch.

"Maybe we need kindling?" Anya suggested. "Ya know, something to get it started? This wood is kinda damp."

A lightbulb went off over Rochelle's head. "Didn't you say you brought magazines?" she asked Liberty. "We could use the paper to start the fire."

Liberty motioned toward her backpack. "If you must . . ."

It took Bria another twenty minutes, but the sticks finally sparked and the pages burst into flames. As the sun set, they gathered around a roaring fire. It was warm and cozy.

"I wish I had some s'mores to roast," Anya said.

"Don't look at me," Liberty said, propping her knee up on her lamb Pillow Pet. "I gave you all the chocolate I had."

Scarlett dug in the bottom of her bag. "I still have a banana. Anyone got something that would go well with it?"

Gracie held up a ketchup packet that had been crammed in her jacket pocket. "How 'bout this?"

"That would be great with my potato chips," Bria suggested. "Chips and dip!"

"I have a little trail mix left," Rochelle said. "How 'bout we sprinkle some nuts and granola on your banana?"

It wasn't exactly a gourmet dinner, but it was a fun feast that they had created together.

"Who wants to tell scary stories?" Rochelle asked.

"Not me," Gracie said, hugging her stuffed pig. "I hate scary stories."

"Oh, good . . . Then I'll go first!" Liberty smirked. "Once upon a time, there was a fabulous and very fashionable ballerina . . ."

Rochelle rolled her eyes. "Seriously? I said a scary story. Not your *E! True Hollywood Story*."

"I'm getting there," Liberty protested. She cleared her throat. "As I was saying: Once upon a time, there was a fabulous and very fashionable ballerina. But she led a tragic life. Her evil, rotten, wicked-witch dance teacher put her high up in a tower where no one could see her loveliness."

"That's Rapunzel," Gracie said. "I saw that movie like a million times."

Liberty placed her hand over Gracie's mouth. "Let me finish! Anyway, this beautiful ballerina spent all her days and nights captive in the tower, until one day, she heard a strange noise below her window."

"Was it the evil wicked witch?" Gracie asked.

"Worse!" Liberty replied. "It was the Creature from the Rock Lagoon and it burped fire and smelled like moldy cheese . . ."

"Watch it," Rochelle warned her. "Unless you want me to fix your other knee . . ."

Liberty kept right on going, unfazed. "This monster was hideous. It had snakes for hair and yellow eyes that gleamed in the darkness. And when she found out the beautiful ballerina was trapped inside, she offered her a deal: trade me your beauty and I will set you free."

Bria mulled over the story. "Let me get this straight: the ballerina has to become the hideous Rock Monster to escape? Oh, that's good . . ."

Rochelle pulled her hood over her ears. "I am not listening to this. It's ridiculous."

"The Rock Monster promised the change in appearance would not be permanent. She would return the ballerina to her original gorgeousness if she would do one tiny little thing for her."

"What? What?" Gracie asked anxiously.

"Slay the wicked witch!"

Anya raised her hand. "Okay, let me get this straight. The ballerina has to give up her beauty and take down the wicked witch? What's in it for her?"

"Freedom!" Liberty replied. "She never has to listen to that witch nag her ever again."

"Of course there's a catch," Scarlett guessed. "Like it's impossible to kill the witch? Or you need some crazy spell and eye of newt to do it?"

"Nope," Liberty replied. "All the ballerina has to do is click her toe shoes together three times and say, 'There's no place like home. There's no place like home.' "

Gracie scratched her head. "That's *The Wizard of Oz*. This story is really mixed up."

"You mean Liberty is really mixed up," Rochelle complained. "I say the Rock Monster should climb up the tower and eat the ballerina for dinner in one big GULP!"

"*Noooo!*" Gracie squealed covering her ears. "That's too scary! I like Liberty's story much better. Tell us how it ends."

"Well, of course the beautiful ballerina outsmarts the Rock Monster. She tells the monster she'll give up her beauty and when the monster unlocks the door to the tower, the ballerina is too quick for her. She runs off and leaves the monster there, hungry and ugly."

"Unbelievable!" Rock shouted.

"And she kills the evil witch?" Gracie asked.

"Worse. She banishes her to a remote forest where she must wander the dark, dusty trails for eternity."

Gracie clapped. "I love it! It could be a Disney movie!"

Liberty smiled. "And the beautiful ballerina lived happily ever after in a Beverly Hills mansion with her billionaire Prince Charming. The end."

Scarlett, Anya, and Rochelle all groaned, but Bria was impressed. "I need to do an original short story for my English class," she said. "Think I can use that?"

"Sorry. Copyright Liberty Montgomery, Inc.," Liberty replied. "Get your own fairy tale."

"I have a better idea," Scarlett suggested. "Let's all sing a song around the fire. How about 'Home on the Range'?"

“Can we jazz it up or something?” Rochelle suggested. “It needs a little Diva rewrite.” She began drumming on her backpack: “*Home, home, yes, home on the range, where the Divas dance and we don’t need a stage . . .*”

“*Buffalo? No! Not a deer in sight,*” Bria improvised. “*Merry Divas to all and to all a good night!*”

Scarlett laughed. “Well, that wasn’t *exactly* what I was thinking, but it works.” She gazed up at the stars. She’d never seen so many before. “Ya know, this isn’t so bad. I thought this trip would be awful. But we all pitched in; we’re all getting along.”

“And there aren’t any werewolves.” Bria breathed a sigh of relief.

But she spoke too soon. A strange howling sound echoed through the woods: “*A-woooooo!*”

“What was that?” Bria said, grabbing Scarlett’s arm. She dug her nails in until Scarlett yelped. “Did you hear that?”

“It was probably just the wind whistling through the trees,” Rochelle tried to convince Bria and herself at the same time.

The howl came again—but this time it sounded louder and closer. "A-*wooooo!*"

"It's a werewolf!" Bria screamed. "Everyone, quick! Into the tent!" They grabbed their sleeping bags and piled inside, leaving Liberty still seated at the fire.

"Hey! What about me? Someone help me up!" she called, trying to crawl her way to the tent. "I can't stand up, remember?"

Bria quickly zipped the tent shut, forgetting that her teammate was still outside.

"Let me in!" Liberty screamed. "Quick! The werewolf is coming!"

CHAPTER 15

Whooooo Goes There?

The girls were panicking when they suddenly realized Liberty was still outside, screaming.

"Hurry up! Let her in!" Scarlett said, pushing Rochelle toward the zipper on the tent.

"Let me think about that for a sec . . ." Rochelle hesitated. "I mean, she did call me a hideous monster who smells like moldy cheese."

Scarlett grabbed her around the shoulders. "Rock! This is a life-and-death situation! Open the tent!"

Rochelle unzipped the flap and pulled Liberty inside.

"Oh my gosh! That was so close!" Liberty said,

hugging Rochelle tightly. The tent was dark and she could barely see a thing.

"Take it easy," Rochelle replied, squirming. "You're okay."

"Ick! Did I just hug you?" Liberty said. "Let go!" She backed away, and felt something long and slithery fall across her shoulder. "*Eek!* A snake! It's a snake! It's choking me! Help!"

Liberty grabbed Rochelle.

Rochelle grabbed Anya.

Gracie tripped over Bria and landed on top of Scarlett.

Rochelle tried to open the front panel of the tent, but the zipper was jammed. She panicked and pushed with all her might until the tent's poles came apart and the entire thing collapsed on top of them. As they scrambled to escape, Bria found the flashlight app on her phone. She shined it right in Liberty's face. "Is everyone okay?" she asked breathlessly.

"I was attacked by a king cobra!" Liberty cried. "How do you think I am? I'm lucky to be alive!"

Bria held the flashlight up to Liberty's neck. "Is this your snake?" she asked, holding up the shoulder strap of Rochelle's bag.

"Well, it felt like snake skin," she said, flicking the bag away.

"It's pleather," Rochelle said, laughing. "Liberty, you are such a wimp!"

Liberty stood up, dusted herself off, and stared Rochelle straight in the eye. "I am not a wimp," she fumed.

"And you're also not hurt anymore." Anya pointed to Liberty's bruised knee. "You can stand up!"

Scarlett giggled. "It's a miracle, Liberty."

Liberty shook her knee out. It did feel much better. Even she had to smile with relief. "Wow. I guess I forgot all about it when the werewolf and snake attacked me. I'm a lot braver than I thought."

"I don't think it was a werewolf," Gracie said, pointing to a high tree branch just above the tent.

A small gray owl was perched on it, gazing dreamily into the light of the full moon. "A-*woooo!*" it hooted.

"He's so cute!" Gracie cooed. "Can we take him home as a friend for Mr. Mustard?"

"I guess we overreacted a little." Bria sighed.

"Ya think?" Rochelle said, laughing. "And what's with the 'we' business? You were the one who made a beeline for the tent to escape Taylor Lautner's bite."

"If it was Taylor Lautner, I would not have run away." Bria giggled. "He's one werewolf I would be okay meeting!"

"Mommy says there's no such thing as werewolves," Gracie insisted. "She says they are just thinkments of our imagination."

"You mean figments," Bria corrected her. "But I get what you're saying, Gracie. I let my imagination run wild."

Liberty shrugged. "Me, too. But when you're in the wild I guess that's the place to do it."

"The point is you're all okay and you all

worked together," said a voice in the darkness. It was no werewolf.

"Miss Toni!" Gracie ran to her teacher and threw her arms around her waist. "Boy, are we glad to see you!"

"I don't know. You girls looked like you were doing pretty well without my help. Except for the falling-tent episode."

"But we did need your help when Liberty got hurt," Scarlett said. "I blew the whistle and you didn't come."

"We were watching everything. We were never more than a few feet behind you," Ranger Sam explained. "I'm an expert at camouflage."

"And I knew Liberty would survive a skinned knee," Toni said and winked. "But it was fun to see you all take turns carrying her down the trail. And I truly enjoyed the choreography down the path and across the stream. Though the wicked-witch dance-teacher tale I could have lived without . . ."

Liberty gulped. "You know I was just kidding, right?"

Gracie tugged on her teacher's sleeve. "I built the tent, but it kinda fell down when the werewolf and poison snake showed up," she told her.

Ranger Sam looked confused. "Werewolves and poisonous snakes? At Black Boulder? I don't think so, girls."

"Do you need a hand putting it back together?" Toni offered. She bent down to pick up the broken pieces of the tent.

"Nuh-uh," Gracie insisted. "We can do it."

Toni looked at her team. They were dirty, battered, and bruised, but they had stuck together. She was proud of them. "I do believe you can. But at least take this." She tossed Scarlett a bag of marshmallows. "It's not a campfire without a marshmallow roast," she said. "See you girls in the morning, bright and early."

"We're going back home?" Bria asked. She'd never missed her mom, dad, and sister so much. She didn't even mind if there were textbooks and homework waiting for her on her desk. All she could picture was her warm, comfy bed and a nice, hot bubble bath.

"I miss Mr. Mustard," Gracie said. "I can't wait to see his furry little face."

"I miss my closet," Liberty added. "I can't wait to get into something that's not wrinkled or stained."

"We are going home—but we have a short stop to make before we do. We're going to a little dance competition in Millville called Curtains Up, and this time, my bathing beauties are going to take home first place."

She didn't have to say it—every Diva could read her mind:

"Or else!"

CHAPTER 16

Bouncing Back

Curtains Up wasn't one of the big, splashy dance competitions that Toni usually chose for her elite team. It was small with only a handful of local studios competing. But it was the perfect place to put to work everything the Divas had learned on their wilderness adventure.

This time, when they took to the stage for the Junior Small Group category, the Divas had a whole new attitude. No one complained about itchy costumes or balloon-like bloomers. They were there to prove to Miss Toni—and to themselves—that they could perform as a team.

Scarlett reviewed the order of who would toss the ball and who would catch it. "Rock, you've got it first, and you hand it off during your *passé* to Bria. Then from Bria it goes down the back row to Anya and she tosses it to Gracie, who is front and center."

Gracie loved her part. She felt like a seal in the circus. She had to balance the ball on her toes during a chin stand, and Scarlett had to scoop it up for a final pass to Liberty.

"How's your knee feeling, Liberty?" Scarlett asked her teammate.

Liberty seemed shocked that anyone cared. "Um, okay I guess." Ranger Sam had done a proper dressing, and it felt just a little tender, but not too stiff anymore.

"Do you think you can do the *fouettés*? If not, we can cover for you," Rochelle offered.

"No! I can do it," she snapped back. Then her face softened. "I mean, I'm okay—thanks for offering."

Scarlett wasn't sure how long all this goodwill

and politeness would last, but she hoped it would hang in long enough for them to dance.

When the announcer called them to the stage, they strutted out confidently. The music began to play and Rock twirled around the stage with the beach ball in her hands. Her *grand jeté* was breathtaking—even better than it had been when she leaped across the stream on the camping trip. The ball floated effortlessly through the air—as if it was dancing, too. The last pose called for all the girls to roll into the "waves" and Liberty to hold the ball over her head as she executed a flawless *développé*. The audience was on their feet cheering, but the only person Scarlett saw was Miss Toni. She was smiling, not just one of her usual tight-lipped semismiles, but a full-on grin from ear to ear.

It was no surprise that when the announcer read the first prize for Junior Small Group Dance, it went to the Dance Divas. Gracie ran up to accept it and blew kisses to the crowd. Miss Toni was already waiting for them in the dressing room when they marched in with the trophy.

"I knew you could do it," she said simply. "I saw a few bobbles here and there, but over-all, it was an outstanding performance. And I hope you've all learned something from this experience."

Anya went over to Bria. "I'm sorry I was so negative about the costumes—and I ruined all the hard work you put into mine."

"It's okay," Bria replied. "I guess I went a little overboard."

Anya dug a blue bow hair clip out of her dance bag. It was studded with stars. "I made you this," she said. "It's all the stars that were left on my costume."

"I love it!" Bria cried, hugging her. "You made this? I didn't know you could sew!"

"You didn't ask," Anya pointed out.

"Sorry. Next time, we make the costumes together—promise!"

Since everyone was apologizing and putting their differences behind them, Scarlett went over to her little sister, who was posing for pictures with the huge gold trophy cup. "Gracie, I've been thinking," she began. "It's okay if we name the kitten Mr. Mustard. If it means that much to you, I can live with it."

"Really?" Gracie asked. "That would be awesome, Scoot. He really loves his name."

"Gracie, do you have something you'd like to say to Scarlett?" Toni asked.

Gracie nodded nervously. "I'm sorry I took your tights. And your leotard. And your hair bows . . . Oh, and your new issue of *Dance* magazine. I cut out some of the ballerina pictures for my mirror."

Scarlett took a deep breath. "I didn't read the new issue yet, but thank you for telling the truth," she said. "And can we agree that you'll *ask* me anytime you want to borrow my stuff from now on?"

"I think that's a fair request," Toni said. "Teammates respect each other's feelings and each other's belongings."

Gracie handed Scarlett back her pink lip gloss. "I took this without asking you, but you can have it back. I'm sorry," shc said.

"Nah, keep it," Scarlett replied. "It's yours now." Her sister's face lit up, and Toni gave them both a thumbs-up.

Gracie might be annoying sometimes, Scarlett thought, *but we will always be teammates and sisters.* And that was pretty much the same thing in her book.

Glossary of Dance Terms

Arabesque: a move where the dancer stands on one leg with the other leg extended behind her at 90 degrees.

Cambre back: a bend from the waist to the back.

Chaîné: a series of quick turns.

Développé: a move where the dancer unfolds her leg in the air.

Fouetté: a turning step where the leg whips out to the side.

Grand jeté: a large forward leap in the air that looks like a flying split.

Pas de bourrée: a move involving three quick steps.

Passé: a move in which the working foot passes close to the knee of the standing leg.

Pirouette: a turn on one leg with the other leg behind.

Relevé: to rise up on pointe or on demi-pointe.

Sheryl Berk is a proud ballet mom and a *New York Times* bestselling author. She has collaborated with numerous celebrities on their memoirs, including Britney Spears, *Glee*'s Jenna Ushkowitz, and *Shake It Up*'s Zendaya. Her book with Bethany Hamilton, *Soul Surfer*, hit #1 on the *New York Times* bestseller list and became a major motion picture. She is also the author of The Cupcake Club book series with her daughter, Carrie.